Betrothed to the Beast

Reformed Rogues, Volume 1

Elina Emerald

Published by Elina Emerald, 2021.

Copyright

Copyright © 2020 by **Elina Emerald**
Betrothed to the Beast

Publisher Elina Emerald / F.Taito. All rights reserved. No part of this publication may be reproduced, distributed, or transmitted in any form or by any means, including photocopying, recording, or other electronic or mechanical methods, without the prior written permission of the publisher, except with brief quotations embodied in critical reviews and certain other noncommercial uses permitted by copyright law. For permission requests contact info@elinaemerald.com or visit www.elinaemerald.com

Disclaimer: This is a work of fiction. Although some characters are based on true historical figures and time periods, their depictions are fictitious.

Cover design by 100covers

Table of Contents

Dedication 1
Thanks 2
Chapter 1 3
Chapter 2 7
Chapter 3 14
Chapter 4 21
Chapter 5 24
Chapter 6 37
Chapter 7 48
Chapter 8 59
Chapter 9 70
Chapter 10 83
Chapter 11 94
Chapter 12 101
Chapter 13 110
Chapter 14 128
Chapter 15 135
Chapter 16 139
Chapter 17 153
Chapter 18 158
Chapter 19 171
Chapter 20 184
Chapter 21 202
Chapter 22 207
Epilogue 217
Author Notes 225

Dedication

To those who believed I would write a book someday.

Thanks

No Writer is an Island

My family, who love me and encourage me to write even though they are not romance fans. In fact, they hate it and would never read this book, but that is beside the point. I still love you.

Melissa. S for keeping me accountable and asking me every day if I have finished the book yet. The answer is yes.

JT Kingsford for being an awesome 'writer catchups' friend and encouraging me to finish something. Beiste also thanks you for talking me out of calling him, Gabriel.

Leilani. W for being so excited about this story before I even knew where it would take me.

Deb. R for being so excited about the book cover.

V. Arya for reminding me that, "Every writer gets bad book reviews so publish it anyway."

Angelina. C for becoming the future inventor of the highly essential "Oh la la" emoji.

Bro O — just because.

Chapter 1

Healers Cottage, Dunbar, East Lothian, Scotland 1033

Impending death has a smell. Amelia knew this to be true, as the metallic scent of blood overpowered the aromatic herbs that had since lost their potency. She sat in stillness while the midwife bustled around the mud-brick room, her heavy steps leaving footprints on the dirt floor. A cloying haze of smoke and steam from boiling water settled mid-air as lingering sweat and strange odors combined to herald a body giving up its right to life.

Amelia had lived fifteen summers and knew that nothing, not the *yarrow* nor the *crushed bog myrtle*, could staunch the bleeding. Her mother, Iona, would be dead within the hour.

She gazed upon the bed where her mother clung to the still-born body of her baby son. Another bastard for the Earl of Dunbar. Amelia reached out and touched his tiny lifeless fingers; it was then she wept for losing a brother she would never know, and a parent she could not bear to let go. If she had not sensed the shift before, she felt it now. The veil between the two worlds was lifting. The midwife made the sign of the cross, then left the cottage.

"Amie," her mother rasped. "Dinnae cry *mo nighean*." Iona moved an errant curl away from Amelia's face. A gesture that exhausted her.

Amelia shook her head in anguish. "No, Ma, please dinnae leave me. I need you."

"Tis my time to go, Love."

"What will I do without you?" Amelia sobbed.

"Use your gift. Your healing skills will see you through." Iona's breathing became labored, but she pushed on between breaths. "I've left you my notes. Tell no one you can read, you ken?" She coughed.

Amelia motioned as if to get water.

"No." Iona clutched Amelia's arm. "There is a letter in my notes and a box for you in the woods. You will need the contents to find your kin. Show it only to them."

"What do you mean? You are my only kin."

"No lass, Highland blood flows through your veins." Iona was wheezing now and gasping for air. "Promise me, you'll find them, tis my gift to you."

"Ma, I dinnae understand."

Her mother winced. "Tell them Iona sent you. Promise me!"

"I promise Ma."

Iona released her grip on Amelia's arm. Her hand lay limp on the bed.

Moments later, the door opened, and Amelia's father, Maldred, Earl of Dunbar, appeared. His facial expression was haggard and etched in sorrow. Maldred collapsed by the bedside.

"Iona, *mo ghràidh,* I am sorry," he said. He then held the hand of his beloved leman as she took her last breath.

Amelia had never seen him cry before. Their eyes met, hers full of anguish and his filled with grief and regret.

"I'm sorry, Lia, I swear to you I will do my best for you. I swear it," he said. With those parting words, Maldred stood and left the cottage.

It would be several days before Amelia retrieved the box buried beneath the hallowed tree. It was made of solid oak. Within it lay a folded *airisaidh* and a crest badge with an insignia on it. A battle axe encircled by branches with the Latin inscription, *"Aut Vincere Aut Mori" - Either Conquer or Die.*

With her heart lighter than it had been in days, Amelia placed the contents back in the box and tucked it under her arm. Somewhere out there in the Highlands, she had a family and someday she would leave this cursed town and find them.

Dunbar Castle, East Lothian — 1040

IF THERE WAS ONE THING Amelia Dunbar knew, it was this; she was never leaving this godforsaken place. After her mother's death, she found herself tied to the estate with never-ending duties as a clan healer. In addition, Amelia still did not know who her kin were because all inquiries had come to a dead-end. And to make matters worse, her father was at this very moment trying to marry her off to a stinking farmer.

Now, by referring to him as such, she did not mean to mock farmers because working with the land is a noble profession. It was the fact said farmer literally stunk. She could smell him from where she stood, and that was a good ten feet away, with the wind blowing in the opposite direction. His name was Angus. He was just shy of forty-nine, with a receding hairline, and every third tooth was rotten or missing. He also had seven children from two deceased wives who had no doubt expired from the stench of his breath.

Amelia knew she was no brilliant catch herself. She was not bonnie or graceful or slim like other women her age, but for the love of all things holy, was it too much to ask that a prospective suitor bathed more than once a year?

"So, what think you, Lia?" the Earl asked. "He's a fine catch with fertile land and lots of cattle."

"I'm sorry Da, but no. I dinnae think Angus and I will get along at all." Amelia waved at Angus, saying a quick "sorry," then walked away.

Exasperated, the Earl followed behind her. "Come now Lia, this is the fifth man you have turned down in two years? I am trying to do my *best* for you. I promised your *màthair* on her deathbed."

That was the part Amelia hated the most. Her father's *best* was not good enough. Her mother became a pariah because of his best. His best caused his wife, Ealdgyth, to die of heartbreak because he could not keep their marriage vows. His best meant Amelia had to take on more duties because he was rarely home. At two and twenty years old, Amelia was sick to death of her father's *best*.

Chapter 2

MacGregor Keep, Glenorchy, Perthshire, Scotland 1040

Chieftain Beiste MacGregor stood on the rocky outcrop, watching his men spar on the training grounds below. He was six foot five of pure muscle, with broad shoulders and a menacing scowl. A hardened warrior, his body bore the visible signs of battle, including a grotesque scar etched across the left side of his face from temple to chin. His bronzed skin was a vivid contrast against rolling green hills. At nine and twenty, Beiste had spent the better part of a decade fighting the wars of kings and now, he just wanted peace.

On Beiste's right hand stood the equally enormous form of his Head-Guardsman, Brodie Fletcher, and to his left was his Second-in-Command, Dalziel Robertson. Brodic was the charmer of their group, with his handsome features and friendly disposition, but rile his temper, and he was as ferocious as a bear. Dalziel was the quiet one, a keen observer. He was leaner than the other two, but twice as deadly.

The three men had fostered together from boyhood and over the years had forged a kinship bond stronger than any blood tie. Ever vigilant, ever alert, they waited in silence for Beiste to speak.

"King Duncan mac Crìonain is dead."

Brodie wiped the smile from his face. "How?"

"Slain in battle by his cousin, Macbeth mac Findlaích."

"A family feud?" Dalziel asked.

"Aye, Thorfinn Sigurdsson of Orkney, aided him."

"I take it Macbeth is now king of Alba," Dalziel asked.

"Aye, twas he who sent the King's missive requiring my immediate action."

"What does he want with you?" Brodie asked.

"I am to marry some wench from the lowlands."

"What?" Brodie looked outraged. "Surely he cannot ask that of you?"

Dalziel agreed. "Tis a low blow. Everyone kens you still mourn your wife."

Beiste did not need reminding. It had been two years, but the memory of Caitrin's death haunted him still.

"He can and he has," Beiste said with anger.

"But why?"

"Because she is Duncan's niece."

"Why would he make you marry the niece of the king he just killed?" Dalziel asked.

"I dinnae ken, but if I refuse, we forfeit our lands."

The men were silent, processing their options.

"And what of Elora?" Brodie asked.

"What of her?"

"Does she ken you mean to take a wife?"

"What I do is none of her concern."

"Are you sure about that?" Brodie looked doubtful.

"Aye!" Beiste snapped. "Women have no say over what I do in or out of bed."

Brodie dropped the subject and glanced at Dalziel, who said nothing. They both knew Elora would not welcome the news.

Dalziel asked, "When must this be done?"

"Within the fortnight."

"Then we best prepare our men. Tis a sennight's ride to the lowlands," Brodie said.

"But first we let off some steam," Beiste replied.

Training Grounds, MacGregor Keep

BEISTE SWUNG HIS BROADSWORD with a feral war cry and ran straight towards his opponent. He had already knocked out several warriors and was in the mood to pummel some more.

Brodie entered the ring and parried the blow with his square-head axe. Now they were locked in combat. Beiste lifted his targe with his right arm and hit Brodie on the left side of his face. Brodie stumbled backward, but not before he swung his axe towards Beiste's head. Beiste blocked the axe with his sword and stepped away.

The two men circled one another. They had been sparring on and off for close to an hour, neither one tiring nor admitting defeat. Brodie swiped his axe again, this time at Beiste's legs. Beiste jumped over it as it sliced through the air. He landed on his feet and, in a surprise move, sprinted headfirst and shoulder-charged Brodie.

The force pushed Brodie backward so fast he lost his footing, landing flat on his back and winded. Before Brodie could roll away, the tip of Beiste's sword was suspended and aimed two inches above his neck.

"Do you yield?" Beiste asked.

"Damn," Brodie replied. He hated losing.

Beiste threw his sword and targe on the ground and offered a hand to Brodie. "Truce?"

Brodie agreed and just as Beiste stepped forward, Brodie swiped his legs out from under him. Both men now lay on their backs, blinking up at the sky. It was then Brodie chuckled and said, "Truce."

They lay on the ground for a moment, trying to catch their breath, when Dalziel appeared in their line of vision and threw a bucket of cold water over them. "Get up, lassies, we have packing to do," Dalziel said, then sauntered away.

"That bastard really needs a good swiving," Brodie grumbled as he and Beiste stood up, shaking the water from their hair and wiping the dust from their trews.

When they turned to face their men, there was a wall of women instead.

Beiste just scowled and walked away in search of water. Brodie spread his arms wide to greet them, his face split into a fierce grin. "Ladies, I need to quench my insatiable thirst!" he shouted.

Brodie was inundated with a bevy of females offering him water cups. He took one and gulped it down, deliberately flexing his muscles in the process to show his side profile to advantage.

"You are so braw and strong, Brodie Fletcher," sighed one young lass.

"That I am minx, braw and strong... all over." Brodie glanced down at his groin, then back at her and winked. She blushed and giggled.

A voluptuous brunette then approached Brodie. She smiled when he turned towards her. Holding her bucket of water, she purred, "I offer you the essence of my pail and anything else you wish to partake of, Brodie Fletcher."

Brodie's smile grew even wider. He could not quite remember her name, but he knew he would take her up on that offer later that night.

Beiste was glad to be away from Brodie's harem. Having women fawn all over him was not something he encouraged. He preferred his women wanton in bed and non-existent outside of it. He could not understand Brodie's need to charm and seduce every woman within a ten-mile radius. Women were too much effort.

Morag the *Cailleach*

IT WAS A FEW HOURS later, the Keep staff and tradespeople were preparing provisions for their chieftain's journey. Dalziel, who was to remain and rule in Beiste's absence, was going over security changes, and Beiste and his War Band of thirty retainers were readying their horses and making final preparations.

Beiste was grooming his destrier *Lucifer* when all chatter ceased as men stared at a point behind him. Some made the sign of the cross, others averted their eyes as the hobbled figure waited. Beiste looked over his shoulder and stared at the wizened form of Morag Buchanan. Her face marred with wrinkles, her hair grey, and the color of her eyes were white. She wore her signature cloak. It was grey like the mist. The men called her *'Oracle.'* Some called her the *Cailleach* or the *hag*, for it was rumored she had the sight. But Beiste had never paid mind to superstition.

"It seems the witch wants a word with you, Chief." Kieran, one of his warriors, gestured towards Morag.

"Aye, t'would seem so." Beiste sighed. He put down the grooming brush and turned to face her. He really did not have time for any of her predictions, but he would hear her out.

"What can I do for you, Morag?" he asked.

"You go to collect your wife, I hear."

"Aye, on the morrow, but she is my betrothed, not yet my wife."

"Whether tomorrow or the next, she is your wife already chosen."

"Is there something you need Morag for I am hard-pressed for time?" He looked impatient.

"Och, you young-uns, you never ken in all your rushing aboot that time has already set her trap for you."

Morag was speaking in riddles again, and Beiste did not have the patience for it. "Well then, Morag, unless you have something important to discuss —."

"Patience Chieftain, I only want to give you these for your men."

Beiste accepted the pouch and jar Morag offered, but he furrowed his brow. "What are these?"

"Tis rose petals and honey."

"Why the bloody hell would my men need roses and honey?"

"Your wife will ken when the time comes." With that, Morag hobbled away, leaning on her staff.

Beiste just looked down at the items and muttered under his breath, "Bloody rose petals?"

"Och and Beiste..."

"What?" he growled.

Her eyes took on an eerie glow, then she said, "Choose well. Our future depends on it."

Elora

IT WAS THE MORNING of their departure, and the men were all gathered in the bailey.

Beiste had taken his leave with his mother, Jonet, and sister, Sorcha. He was just getting the horse tethered when, again; he sensed a movement behind him.

Did every woman in this blasted Keep feel the need to speak to him before he left?

"Elora," he grunted. Her smile faltered at his curt tone. Beiste hated this part of dealing with women who wanted more from him than he agreed to give. Elora had warmed his bed months ago. She was the only woman he had been with since his wife's passing. He found her naked in his bed waiting for him one night and took the pleasure she offered, making no promises in return. Ever since then, she had tried to stake some claim on him.

"I heard you will be gone for a few days," Elora said.

"Aye," Beiste replied, and continued tightening the saddle.

"Were you going to tell me?" She looked irate.

"I dinnae ken why I have to tell you anything, Elora."

"But I need to ken your whereabouts if I am to help run this Keep."

And there it was. Brodie and Dalziel had warned him. Elora had misconstrued their relationship or lack of one.

Beiste stopped and turned to face her. Elora flinched and took a step back. He hated it when a woman cowered before him. He had never, not once, raised his hand to a woman.

"Elora, whatever we had lasted only those two nights, months ago."

"But you've not taken anyone else to your bed, which means you must have developed powerful feelings for me." She pouted.

"Are you daft? That means nothing. We made no promises."

"But I've been keeping myself for you."

"Really?" Beiste raised an eyebrow. "Because I heard you took up with Lachlan three weeks ago."

Elora's eyes grew wide. "How did you ken that?"

"Lachlan asked me what my intentions were towards you, and I told him I had none."

"But I've changed my mind. I dinnae want Lachlan. I want you, Beiste. It has always been you." She flung herself at him and wrapped her arms around his middle.

Saints preserve him. Beiste had had enough. He removed her arms from around his waist and gently but firmly set her away from him. "No!" he replied. Then he focused back on *Lucifer,* already clearing his mind of the woman behind him.

⚜

Chapter 3

Belhaven Village, Dunbar - *Nine days later*

"Come on, Mary! Stop dawdling. We dinnae have time today," Amelia said in exasperated tones as she hurried across the crowded streets of *Belhaven*. One hand clutching a basket now overflowing with seasonal produce, her other hand holding her sister's tunic so as not to lose her in the crowd.

It was Market Day in the village, the busiest day of the month, and there were vendors aplenty. Amelia was there to purchase more seeds for her garden and pick up silks for their *seanmhair*. Unfortunately, Mary, her half-sister, was dragging her feet.

"I dinnae ken why you wouldna let me buy that necklace." Mary pouted. "The vendor said twas a fair price for the quality and it made my blonde curls striking."

Amelia rolled her eyes as they weaved their way through brightly colored baskets of fresh fruit and vegetables. "Mary, he would've said the same thing to a muddy pig if he thought it had coin to spare." Gentling her voice, Amelia tried to placate her sister saying, "Once I get the provisions *Seanmhair* ordered, we can get some berry tarts."

Mary's eyes brightened immediately. "Really? I'm famished."

The promise of sweet treats ahead motivated Mary to pick up her pace.

The sisters passed stalls selling a vast array of items, from soaps and medicinal herbs and spices to fresh flowers and candy apples. Pigs were roasting over open fires, while merchants peddled their wares of silks and materials from exotic places. Amelia was so glad she had dressed in an ankle-length linen tunic. With the warmer weather and crushing crowds, it kept her cool. She had just purchased their freshly baked berry tarts when Mary started waving at someone in the crowd.

"Amelia, I see some of my friends. Can I go sit with them?"

"Who are they, Mary?" Amelia asked.

"Tis the Frasers, Isobel and her brother Patrick. They come every few weeks to trade."

"Very well, but please mind my basket and you can take my tart to share. Tis not polite to eat on your own in front of others."

Mary's eyes lit up. "Thank you, Amie." She hugged her and disappeared into the crowd.

Amelia continued alone to secure the silks for her grandmother when a vendor stepped out in front of her. He gave her a leery look while licking his lips.

"Would you like to come into my tent, lass? I have some cool cider for a pretty one like you." His plaid looked dirty, his hair greasy, and there was an unpleasant odor wafting off him that caused Amelia to almost gag.

Honestly? Amelia thought, *how hard was it to bathe when the North Coast Sea was less than two hundred feet away?*

"No thank you, I dinnae need cider," Amelia politely refused.

He stepped closer to her, crowding her in, and she stepped around him. He was about to lunge at her when the thundering sound of horses was heard through the village. The hairs on the back of her neck stood on end. Even the lecherous vendor turned to look behind him.

Amelia took a deep breath. She could feel something coming, its raw energy warning her as the earth beneath her feet rumbled. She spun around.

The villagers began muttering and grabbing their children. Some huddled behind their stalls, all eyes on the strangers approaching. They were fierce looking; they wore armor and plaid.

Amelia heard a woman gasp, "Tis the MacGregors." They looked as if they had come straight from battle. Then the same woman pointed and cried, "Tis the *Beast*!"

Amelia looked in that direction and saw him. *He was magnificent.* The sheer size of him made her shudder. He emanated raw energy. His bronzed skin and black piercing eyes missed nothing. He wore an angry scowl, made even more menacing by the vicious scar across his face. Men of equal size surrounded him, all wearing the MacGregor plaid. Flanking to his right was an equally fearsome warrior wearing animal fur with a battle axe strapped to his back.

Amelia stood mesmerized at the sight.

It would seem the lecherous vendor had taken the opportunity of Amelia's distraction to lunge for her again. She tried to keep clear of his grip and instead propelled too far forward; the momentum pushing her directly onto the road and into the path of the riders. She froze and knew they would trample her to death, and oh, the regret that she had not even left this miserable sodding town.

Amelia heard a shout ring out from the one they called the Beast; he was riding straight for her. This was it. This was the end. She closed her eyes until she felt a firm arm reach down and sweep her up like she weighed nothing.

She opened her eyes to find herself sitting atop a horse, her bottom wedged between strong thighs. The smell of leather and man rattled her senses as she drank in the heady sensation before he yelled, "Daft, wench! Are you trying to get yourself killed?"

"What?" Amelia whipped her head around to glare at him, but stared at a bare chest instead.

The Beiste tightened his hold on her, slowed his horse, then set her down in the clearing.

She looked up to offer her thanks when he reprimanded her again. "Watch where you walk, silly chit! You could've been hurt or maimed. What were you thinking, just standing in the middle of the road like a stunned cow?" Before Amelia could respond, he continued with his tirade. "Next time do your wool-gathering where it cannot get you bloody killed!"

Outraged that she would receive such a set down by a stranger in a public place, Amelia had had enough. Not only did the big brute call her stupid, he called her a cow. *A cow!* After two and twenty years of having the villagers snicker at her and vile, stinking men grope her, there was no way she was letting an ogre call her a cow.

With both hands firmly on her hips, Amelia let fly. "How dare you? You, big ox! You," — Her finger pointed at him. — "should not ride into a village" — Her finger pointed at the village. — "without a care in the world!" — Both arms went up in the air gesturing the world. — "You could have killed me!" — Both hands went back to her hips — "And just because I have a big arse, it does not make me a cow!" Amelia screeched.

She was out of breath, her face was red after that display and standing on the roadside venting her spleen, she had to admit she felt somewhat better.

In her mind, Amelia believed she had kept a civil yet stern tongue, but when she looked around and found the entire village silent and everyone staring at her with mouths ajar, she realized she had, in fact, been screaming at high volume. Had she taken the time to think about it, she would have kept her mouth shut altogether.

The Beast stared at her for what seemed like an eternity; he raised his hand to signal to his men to stop. They were currently smirking, trying to wipe the amusement from their faces. Beiste dismounted his horse and scowled, his face a mask of tightly controlled rage. He walked towards the woman he now considered a *howling wench* and, given his height and the length of his legs, it took him two seconds to reach her.

Oh bollocks. Amelia's throat suddenly felt parched, she could feel all the villagers behind her step away. She could already hear the bards singing about her death in a marketplace covered in candy apples, berry tarts, and horseshit. For centuries, she would be the cautionary tale for plump Gaelic women everywhere with acerbic tongues. *"Bloody hell!"* she muttered to herself. She was on her own.

As the Beast approached, her knees trembled. She saw his broadsword sheathed in the scabbard at his side.

Was that blood still on his sword? Was that the blood of another mouthy lass who dared to question him in the previous village? The road spun. She felt lightheaded, but she would not yield. Amelia raised her chin slightly. Her mind sifting through escape plans, all of them failing because she could not run without sustaining a serious chafing injury. She was doomed.

Amelia looked up. The Beast was standing directly in front of her, staring down. *Lud, he was huge.* She braced.

"The next time a man saves your life, a word of thanks would do, not your damn screaming like a banshee for the world to hear!" He roared the last part of the line.

"You," — His finger pointed at her. — "are damned lucky my men and I," — His finger pointed at himself and his men. — "dinnae believe in harming women, if you," — He pointed at her again. — "had challenged anyone else," — Both his arms gestured around the village. — "who kens what your insolence could have cost you?" — He pointed at her then brought his face closer. — "Have a care for your safety lass, dinnae court danger with your reckless behavior," he seethed.

Amelia thought, for someone who accused others of screaming, he sure did a lot of bellowing himself.

The Beast looked at a point behind her and shouted, "Is this your woman? If she is, you need to keep a firm hold of her tongue."

A deep voice with a smooth brogue answered, "No, she is not, but I would still prefer no harm came to her."

Amelia whipped her head back to find Mary's friend Patrick Fraser a scant distance behind her, standing legs apart, one hand resting on the scabbard of his sword, as if ready to protect her. *Bless-ed man.* She spotted Mary and Isobel a safe distance away, looking worried. Amelia suddenly felt contrite and embarrassed. *Could this day get any worse?*

"I am sorry. I thank you for saving me," she responded, feeling genuine remorse and relief that the Beast had not taken her head off with his broadsword.

The Beast continued to stare at her for a few moments, then just grunted, shook his head, and walked away.

COULD THIS DAY GET any worse? Beiste could not believe the wee termagant he had just encountered. He was tired and hungry, and that besom screamed at him like a wild, stuck boar when he had just saved her life. The daft woman needed to reign in that temper of hers before she met with violence. It worried him that the bonnie lass was courting danger. *The woman had a death wish.*

Beiste heard a chuckle from his left and gritted his teeth. Brodie the ass found the whole incident amusing and had not stopped chortling about it since they left the village. Beiste instantly regretted his decision to bring Brodie along. The man was an idiot.

As they rode towards Dunbar Castle, Beiste kept thinking on the termagant once more. He noted she looked familiar, a memory from his past, those eyes of hers one brown and one green. He had seen them before. Beiste thought also of her kissable lips and luscious breasts and rounded hips. He had become aroused watching her feisty display.

For a screaming banshee, she had a body built to take an enormous man without fear of breaking her. Beiste shook his head to stop the errant thoughts plaguing his mind. It had been too long since he'd had a woman. He was now lusting after some screeching, *she-cat*. But he would say this; she smelled of lilacs and clean fresh woodlands. If only she was not such a screamer. An even darker thought crossed his mind. What would she be like under him, screaming his name in pleasure? *Damn it!* He needed to stop this train of thought. *Damn wench.*

Chapter 4

Dunbar Castle, East Lothian

Back at the castle, Amelia and Mary had just entered through the kitchens when they were accosted by their *seanmhair*, Lady Agnes.

"Amelia, where have you two been?"

"We were at the markets, Grandma. I have all the provisions you requested."

"Aye, Grandma, we would have been here earlier, but Amelia had a bit of a disagreement with —"

"Hush Mary! No one has time for your stories. There is someone here to see you. He is from the King," Lady Agnes said.

"The King?" the sisters repeated.

Lady Agnes grabbed Mary's hand and yelled at Amelia to follow. She was pulling Mary up the stairs to her bedchamber and shouting orders at serving women for hot water and soap and curling irons and kirtles.

"Grandma, what is happening?" Amelia asked breathlessly, trying to keep up.

"The new king has betrothed Mary to the MacGregor chieftain, and he's downstairs."

"What?" the sisters shouted.

"Please tell me it's not true?" Mary wailed.

"When was this arranged?" Amelia asked.

"Your uncle, Duncan, has gone and gotten himself killed the silly man. Your Da is trying to make sense of the parchments."

"But what has that to do with Mary?" Amelia asked, now gasping for air as she climbed more stairs.said

"We are Duncan's closest kin, and that Macbeth is trying to bring us to heel," Lady Agnes replied. Her expression was a combination of grief and anger. She kept running up the stairs, showing far more agility than both of her granddaughters. She did not pause once. Meanwhile, Amelia had given up breathing altogether.

Once inside the room, Lady Agnes issued orders. "Amelia, get Mary into that bath. Mary, stop crying. You look hideous. Where are the hairbrushes, Hilde?" The lady's maid and servants were scurrying around like frightened mice. "Amelia, set out the gold dress."

"Aye, Grandma."

"And Amelia, I want you to go bathe. Hilde will help you. There's a plain kirtle set out for you to wear."

"Why do I need to get ready?" Amelia gave her a questioning look.

"Stop bothering me with your ceaseless chatter child, just do as I say!"

Twenty minutes later, the sisters were bathed and dressed. Mary wore the Dunbar *airisaidh* over her kirtle fastened by an heirloom silver brooch.

Lady Agnes said, "Mary, you will go downstairs and meet your betrothed. You will smile and be charming and you will stop crying this instant."

Mary nodded, then burst into tears again.

"By the saints, I canna stomach hysterical women," Lady Agnes declared.

"Amelia, you will stand beside Mary for support."

Amelia interrupted her. "Mayhap Grandma it would be better if I just went to my cottage and did not go to the hall."

"No, you cannot leave me, Amelia." Mary started panicking.

"But Mary, if it's the same man from the village, I could make it worse," Amelia replied.

"Why would you make it worse?" Lady Agnes raised an eyebrow.

"Well, I may have had a wee run-in with their leader."

"What kind of run-in?" Lady Agnes demanded.

"Amelia yelled at him in the village," Mary replied and sniffed.

"I would not say I yelled, Mary."

"Screamed then."

"No, I did not scream at him, Mary."

"Bellowed then."

"No, I did not bellow at him either, Mary."

"Screeched then."

"*Wheesht* Mary! I didna raise my voice at all," Amelia shouted.

"Oh, you mean how you're not raising your voice now?" Mary smirked.

"At least I'm not marrying him," Amelia retorted.

Mary began wailing even louder.

"Saints preserve us, that is enough. Am I the only person in this bloody castle trying to keep a clear head?" Lady Agnes was nearing the end of her patience. She turned to Amelia and said, "It does not matter what you said to their leader, he will only have eyes for Mary."

Amelia pleaded with her grandmother in a desperate bid to avoid the MacGregors. "But Grandma, I should be at the cottage picking the final sundew for the bairns. They could die from whooping cough in winter."

"Enough Amelia! Pick the blasted sundew tomorrow. Bairns will not be perishing overnight for lack of sundew. You will go with Mary to the hall, and you will pass me that whiskey bottle. I need to fortify my spirit."

Chapter 5

The Great Hall, Dunbar Castle

The Betrothal

Beiste stood in the center of the Great Hall with his eyes fixed on the main doors. His hair was partially wet from having bathed in the sea. He wore his proper MacGregor plaid with a crest badge. The look on his face was one of annoyance and contempt.

As the Earl prattled on to Brodie about Royal Burgh matters, Beiste remained still, silent, calm. He was impatient. Another hour had passed, and he was not in the mood for polite conversation. *What could take the chit so long?* The sooner this betrothal was done, the sooner he could return to the Highlands.

As his eyes roamed the Great Hall, it was easy to see the affluence of the occupants. The Dunbars remained a powerful clan with their Cumbrian connections despite their castle being burnt down several times, once by a MacAlpin. Beiste wondered how many other useless historical facts he could recall before he finally set eyes on this Mary woman. As if his thoughts had summoned her, a loud commotion came from the primary entrance as three women entered the Great Hall. *About time!*

Beiste deduced from the look of them it was Lady Agnes, the Earl's mother, and the woman following behind her would be his betrothed. His face remained expressionless as he casually observed their approach.

The blonde lass was a beauty. She wore the Dunbar *airisaidh* over a golden kirtle, which accentuated her slim, lithe figure. But his eyes were drawn to the brunette walking beside her. She wore a long brown linen tunic with a simple white *airisaidh*. Her hair was a riot of dark brown curls. She kept her head down, but he knew full well who she was.

It was that same infuriating lass he had encountered in the village. For some unknown reason, it annoyed him. He just got her out of his head and there she was again, tempting his resolve.

Beiste glared at Lady Agnes as if it was her fault.

Seeing Beiste's expression, Lady Agnes faltered and hesitated to approach further.

Brodie elbowed Beiste in the ribs and whispered through gritted teeth, "For goodness' sake, smile, or you'll scare the women away."

Beiste growled, "I dinnae care!"

Brodie rolled his eyes and muttered under his breath, "You can be a real prick sometimes." Brodie gave the women his most charming smile, hoping to put them at ease. It had the required effect as they resumed their approach. When they reached the dais, the Earl began the formal introductions.

"Chieftain MacGregor, Brodie Fletcher. May I introduce my *màthair*, Lady Agnes?"

She greeted the men with a slight curtsy, then beckoned the blonde lass over. "I ken you are most eager to meet your betrothed. May I present my *ban-ogha*, Lady Mary?"

Giving Mary a stern look, Lady Agnes directed her towards Beiste.

Mary reluctantly stepped forward and greeted Beiste with a cautious smile. But he caught her momentary grimace when she viewed his facial scar. It was the same reaction most women had to his disfigurement.

Beiste noticed Lady Agnes pinch Mary's arm. Mary quickly veiled her reaction and greeted him in a timid voice. "Chieftain MacGregor tis happy I am to meet you." Mary then curtsied low and stepped back to stand beside her grandmother. Her lower lip trembled when her grandmother pinched her again.

Damn, the poor lass was here under duress. This did not bode well for a future marriage. Beiste thought.

Amelia stood behind her sister and grandmother and snorted with disgust. She wished she were far away from the dumb brute's presence. Watching him glower and carry on as if everyone was beneath him spoke volumes of his arrogance. She only hoped her father could save Mary from a bleak future.

Preoccupied with her own thoughts, Amelia was unaware that her inelegant snort had gained Beiste's attention and his eyes now rested on her. Although he could not see her face, judging by her rigid stance, he sensed she was angry with him. War had trained Beiste to read the body language of others and at that moment he could tell the little termagant was working herself up into a snit.

With no introduction forthcoming, Beiste broke his veil of disinterest and abruptly asked, "Lady Agnes, who is this lass?" He nodded his head towards Amelia.

All conversation ceased. Mary, who was struggling and failing to make polite conversation, seemed relieved the attention had shifted from her.

"Och, forgive me, this is Amelia. She is Mary's, uh... companion."

Amelia grimaced. As many times as she had heard it over the years, it still stung that they referred to her as a *companion*. That word was a constant reminder that she would never fully belong, no matter how much she did for the Clan.

Amelia was still wool-gathering when Lady Agnes pulled her forward to meet Beiste. Startled out of her reverie, she tripped on the front of her overlong tunic and plummeted headfirst towards the floor.

On instinct, Beiste stepped forward and caught her, pulling her up against his chest.

Amelia lifted her head and froze as a pair of intense obsidian eyes gazed down at her. No one ever looked at her that way before. Something shifted between them. Every part of his body radiated sheer power and shrewd intelligence. Amelia had been wrong about her earlier estimations. This was no dumb brute and lord did he smell clean.

Amelia's eyes then wandered to his scar. Her healer's mind scowled at the brutal hands that had treated it. The gash would have healed better with aloe. She wondered if she had a salve in her stores that could ease the tightness of the skin as she traced her fingers gently across the old wound.

Beiste stared at Amelia's countenance, and it knocked all the breath from his lungs when he felt the shocking sensation of soft fingers tracing the line of his scar. It was an intimate gesture. No woman had ever dared touch his scar. Somewhat astonished, he welcomed her curiosity. He liked the way her touch felt against his skin. She was warmth and softness to his cold hardened heart. In that instant, Beiste was aware of only one person in the room.

"Amelia! Stop touching the chieftain's face!" The Earl's quiet reprimand broke through the intimacy of the moment.

Shocked by her momentary lapse of reason, Amelia apologized, "Forgive me." Her face erupted in a pink flush. She placed both hands on his chest and pushed away.

Beiste reluctantly let her go.

"Amelia, are you all right?" Mary frowned.

Brodie stifled a laugh, diffusing the tension. He winked at Amelia and said, "By all means, lass, you can touch me anytime you like."

Beiste, with fists clenched, made a growling sound at him which had Brodie lifting his hands in surrender and stepping away.

"Have ye taken leave of your senses, child? Keep your hands to yourself," Lady Agnes tsked. "Go on now, get back to your chores." She shooed Amelia away from the dais.

It thrilled Amelia to be excused. She started walking backward, gave a quick curtsy, then she spun around and walked-ran at a brisk pace out the main doors.

Beiste continued to stare at Amelia's retreating form until the doors closed behind her. He did not understand what had happened, but he felt disappointed at her leaving. The buzzing sound coming from his left grew louder as he continued to stare. He turned to find Mary trying to say something to him. He relented and gave her his full attention.

"Will you not come and sit by me for refreshments?" Mary asked as she gestured to a table on the dais. It was lavishly set with silverware, wine and ale, and an assortment of food. It surprised Beiste to look about the hall and see his men were all seated. He had not noticed them at all. He shook his head in disbelief. Never had he been so utterly distracted by a female that he was unaware of his immediate surroundings. This was not good. He made a mental note to wipe the vixen from his mind. He needed to get this betrothal completed and head back to the Highlands.

BEISTE SAT BETWEEN Mary and the Earl for the past two hours and he wanted to kill himself. Mary could barely speak without her lip trembling, and Lady Agnes kept kicking Mary under the table. Beiste knew this because the daft woman often missed and kicked his shin instead. The Earl had imbibed too much ale and was falling asleep, and Brodie was busy flirting with several serving women.

Just when Beiste was thinking of heading back to camp, the doors to the hall burst open and a disheveled, callow man came running inside shouting for help.

Beiste and his men immediately stood on alert when the Earl yelled, "Harold, whatever is the matter?"

Harold twisted the cap he held nervously in his hand and in a panicked voice said, "Forgive the intrusion my lord, but Mistress Amelia seems to have started a war with the Kennedys."

Beiste and his men were already on the move.

The Kennedys

PUSHING ALL THOUGHTS of Beiste from her mind, Amelia returned to her healer's cottage and had no time to contemplate anything else because a woman and her guardsman were waiting for her. The woman wore a long, black, expensive cloak and a black veil covering over her face. She was desperately trying to quieten an unsettled baby.

"Are you Amelia, the healer?" the woman asked.

Amelia recognized her accent as being Northumbrian. She nodded and replied, "Aye."

The woman looked relieved. "Praise be. I am sorry to intrude, but I am desperate for help for my son. I have heard of your skills."

"Come inside." Amelia ushered her into the cottage.

The woman gave instructions to her guard. He remained outside while she followed Amelia indoors.

"Now then, what ails your bairn? What is his name?"

"Thomas. He does not take well to milk. Our healer has tried everything, but he is getting worse. I beg you to help him."

"Aye, come sit down and I'll take a look."

Amelia walked over to a pitcher of water and basin. She washed and dried her hands, then stretched her arms out to take the babe.

She cooed at him as he made gurgling noises and he smiled at her. "Come now Thomas, let me have a look at you." Amelia unwrapped his clothes and saw he looked half-starved. She kept rocking him while feeling his body and looking over his skin as she spoke.

"Tell me what happens when you feed him?"

"A short time after every feed, he cries in pain. His entire body tightens and his stomach swells. He lets out so much wind and his tummy runs. Then he is hungry again and the process repeats. He has lost so much weight. I fear he will waste away."

"How often does this happen?"

"Only after I feed him. I thought it was my milk, but it is the same if I use a wet nurse. I do not know what else to do." With that, she burst into tears.

Amelia reached out her hand to soothe her. "Tis all right. I will do what I can."

The woman lifted the veil, revealing her face. It surprised Amelia at first, but she understood the secrecy.

"I am Eliza Kennedy. I want you to know who it is you help. My husband can be very stubborn and our clans are not on the best terms. But this is our son and I will not watch him die because of his father's pride."

Amelia felt pity for the woman. A mother's love was stronger than a husband's hatred for an enemy. "Tis all right, Thomas is an innocent babe who kens not about the wars of men." Amelia began moving around the cottage, setting a fire, and gathering things for the babe who had fallen asleep. She placed him on a make-shift cot. In between, she asked questions of Eliza regarding Thomas' health.

"Here, take some cider and eat some broth to calm yourself. You need to keep up your strength as well. You look exhausted." Amelia handed the fare to Eliza, then took some cool cider and bread and cheese to the guard outside. Once her guests were settled, she went into her bedchamber and consulted her mother's book of healing notes.

She came out a few minutes later. "I think I ken what ails him, but I will have to try a few things."

Eliza nodded and looked hopeful.

"I just need to source some things from outside."

Behind the Healer's cottage, Amelia had built up an extensive garden of herbs and plants and a large pen where she kept livestock. She filled a pitcher with fresh goat's milk and returned to the cottage. Amelia cut a clean piece of cloth and boiled it in scalding water, then let it cool on a hanging rack. She then warmed the goat's milk in a pot over the fire.

The babe woke and started fussing again. His mother changed him into dry clothes and handed him to Amelia. She cradled him in her arms, dipped the clean cloth into the warm goat's milk, then let the babe suckle the cloth. Thomas suckled the milk from the cloth and stopped crying, then began fussing for more. Amelia repeated the process over and over until the babe had drunk two-thirds of the goat's milk. Thomas looked sleepy as she burped him, then let him sleep. Amelia placed him on the makeshift cot with a soft cover and he slept contentedly.

Eliza anxiously looked on. "What happens now?"

"Now, we wait and see how he fares."

Two hours later, Thomas continued to sleep peacefully.

"He has never slept this long before, especially after a feed," Eliza remarked.

Right on cue, Thomas woke and started fussing, but there was no pain or crying. Eliza gently carried him around the cottage, and he cooed, then smiled and stared around the room.

"I cannot believe it. This has never happened before. Usually, he is screaming by now," Eliza said.

Amelia explained. "There is something in all milk that can cause upset for weak stomachs. Goats' milk has a wee bit less than other forms. I just needed to try it."

"I dinnae ken how I can ever repay you," Eliza replied with watery eyes.

"Just make sure he grows strong, tis payment enough. You are welcome to stay here as long as you need. But remember warm goats' milk dipped in a clean cloth."

After an hour, there was no sign of distress from Thomas, so Amelia felt it was safe to assume her treatment had worked. The two women were laughing and playing with Thomas, who was very much settled and smiling when they heard a tremendous commotion outside.

Ten men surrounded the cottage and one furious Kennedy laird shouted, "Come out, you witch! What have you done to me, wife and son? You evil one."

The guard outside would not let him come closer, and it looked like blood was about to be spilled.

Eliza fretted. "I am so sorry to bring this to your doorstep."

Amelia would not be cowered. She opened the door, still holding a smiling Thomas, and stepped outside but far enough away from the men.

"You witch, why is my son smiling? What smiling spell have you cast on him?" Laird Kennedy yelled.

"Quiet, you annoying man!" Amelia shouted back. He looked stunned at her outburst. "I have done nothing to him. He is smiling because he is happy. Your wife is also hale."

Eliza stepped out of the cottage and said, "Tis true, we are both well. The healer has helped find a cure for our son."

"Eliza, come away from there, Wife. She has bewitched you both. I may need to kill her to break the spell." Laird Kennedy moved closer to the cottage.

"You will do no such thing," Eliza replied. "She saved our son. I will not let you harm her."

Thomas started fussing with the sound of raised voices, so Amelia returned him to Eliza and told them to go inside.

"You will give me back my wife, Witch, or I will burn your cottage to the ground!" the Kennedy laird shouted.

Something about his threat to burn her dead mother's cottage down caused something deep inside Amelia to snap. And for the second time that day, she let fly. "Are you a moron? I am not a witch, and I did not cast a spell on your wife or bairn." Amelia was livid, and she was now on her tiptoes, shouting and pointing her finger directly at him.

"Your son has a weak stomach. I found the milk he could drink to help him grow strong. There is no witchery involved."

"How dare you? My son is not weak and dinnae yell at me. I am a laird!" he hollered in reply.

"Then act like one, you big bairn. Look at you just standing there scaring your wife and babe, you coward!"

"Dinnae call me a coward! You need a firm hand, you bloody witch."

"Come on then you, big baw sack," Amelia taunted and picked up the broom by the door, ready to battle.

"Lass, I dinnae think tis a good idea to challenge the laird," Eliza's guard cautioned her. Even he was questioning the sanity of the woman beside him wielding a broom.

Amelia brushed him off, saying, "Shush! I'm about to go into battle."

BEISTE COULD NOT BELIEVE what he was witnessing at the Healer's cottage. *The woman had a death wish.* Armed men surrounded her in a semi-circle. Their leader was bellowing at her while she held a broom and challenged him to... *battle?*

The sound of their arrival caused the men to turn, and soon the Kennedys were facing off with the MacGregors and the Dunbars.

"Laird Kennedy, why are you on my land?" Maldred shouted.

"Your witch has my wife and child in her clutches."

"I am not a witch, you bloody imbecile!" Amelia screamed, pointing her broom at him.

Beiste could not stomach it anymore. He dismounted, cursing under his breath, and stormed straight towards Amelia. The Kennedy retainers let him through because he had an ominous look on his face. He strode past them. When he reached Amelia, he snatched the broom out of her hand, snapped it in half, and threw it on the ground. Then he stooped and flung her over his shoulder.

"You just broke my broom! I need that broom," she whined while hanging upside down.

Beiste whacked her backside. "Be quiet!"

She instantly quieted.

Beiste turned to face all the men, Amelia dangling over his shoulder. "Nobody bloody move!" he roared. Everyone nodded, including the Kennedy laird. Beiste then walked them into the cottage and slammed the door.

Once inside, Beiste placed Amelia on her feet. "Sit down," he snapped.

She sat down instantly.

"Now what the devil is going on?"

Eliza quickly stood, holding Thomas, and stepped forward. "'Tis my fault. I brought my son to Amelia for healing and my husband is being difficult." At that moment, Thomas gave Beiste a toothless grin.

Beiste's eyes softened momentarily, and he reached out and gave a quick stroke to the babe's cheek.

Amelia and Eliza looked on, surprised at his reaction.

Beiste then turned to Amelia and asked, "Were you able to help the babe?"

"Aye, he should get better now with proper feeding."

Beiste nodded, then turned to Eliza and asked, "Why is your husband being difficult?"

"He has been feuding with the Dunbars for some years now and forbade me to seek Amelia's help."

Beiste looked around the cottage, noticing the vast array of herbs and fresh flowers. *So, she was a healer.* "But you sought her out anyway and now we have the situation outside," he stated matter of fact to Eliza.

"Yes." Eliza looked guilty. "My husband has a short temper, but he is all bluster. I know tis because he worries about us, but he would never really hurt anyone."

"Your husband will get himself killed one day with all that bluster. If he had come onto MacGregor land with ten men threatening one of our women, I would have run him through with no hesitation."

Eliza paled at Beiste's frank appraisal, but she had to admit he had a point.

"And you," —Beiste pointed at Amelia— "you did not help matters with your caterwauling." He gave her a stern look.

Amelia opened her mouth to say something.

"Shut it," he said. So, she did. "Gather whatever the babe and his *màthair* need for the journey home. I will make sure this does not end in bloodshed."

Amelia quickly grabbed a basket thinking now was not the time to argue.

Beiste left the women inside and walked out to address the laird. "Laird Kennedy," he yelled.

"Aye."

"I am Beiste MacGregor, and my clan is allied with the Dunbars. That means my protection extends to anyone on this land."

Laird Kennedy and his men looked around at the huge warriors surrounding them.

"Your wife and son are well, thanks to the healer. They will join you shortly. You have one hour to leave this land. My men will escort you to the boundary line."

The laird nodded. Beiste noticed he was not so vocal now that he was up against men his own size and not facing down a lone woman with a broom.

Beiste added, "And before you take your leave, you will say sorry to the healer for calling her a witch."

"I most certainly will not say sorry." Laird Kennedy looked appalled.

Beiste drew his broadsword, pointed it at the laird and roared, "You will, or I will, cut you down!"

All the MacGregor retainers put their hands to their weapons, ready to back their chieftain.

Laird Kennedy paled and backed down. All bluster gone. "All right. No need to get dramatic," he grumbled.

Beiste stormed back to *Lucifer* and mounted. Turning back towards the castle, he muttered under his breath, "I swear that reckless woman will be the death of me."

Brodie burst out laughing.

Chapter 6

The Obsession

The following morning, Beiste was back at the Great Hall, spending time with Mary before they formalized the betrothal. Brodie, the diplomat, had arranged it with Lady Agnes. Brodie had also emphasized to Beiste he should focus on his betrothed and not her companion.

But try as he might and as bonnie as Mary was, Beiste was disinterested. He still could not get that infuriating healer out of his head. When he had ridden over the hill and seen the men surrounding her cottage, his heart had lodged in his throat. Then to find out she had put herself in danger over a babe, he wanted to flay the skin off that laird. Instead, his only instinct was to remove her from harm's way.

Beiste pitied the poor man she ended up marrying. They would not get a moment's peace. He then scowled at the thought of any man touching her.

"So, what do you think?" Mary asked quizzically.

"About what?"

"Do you believe in true love?"

"No," he replied.

Mary was quiet again and stared at her slippers.

Beiste felt like a brute. She was trying to make conversation. He cleared his throat and said, "I dinnae believe in love. I only believe in duty."

"What if duty is not enough?" Mary asked.

Beiste was silent. He did not quite have an answer for that. He never really thought about it. His marriage to Caitrin was one of duty. It was awkward at first but over time they formed an affection for one another. He would not call it love, but he still mourned when she died.

With nothing much else to say, Beiste excused himself to check on his men. When he arrived at the camp, it surprised him to find most of his War Band missing.

Healers Cottage, Dunbar Estate

THAT AFTERNOON, AMELIA was putting together herbal tea pouches for the women in the village. She was engaged in the repetitive action of scoop and pour and scoop and pour whilst gazing out the window. One thing she was *not* doing was thinking about the Beast.

No, she was *not* thinking about his clean, woodsy scent of leather and musk, or how muscular his shoulder felt against her hips. She was *not* contemplating the muscles in his thighs which rippled with every movement or how her quim spasmed when he stormed towards her and threw her over his shoulder. And there was no way she was acknowledging how often he had featured in her erotic dreams last night. No, not at all.

Amelia Dunbar did *not* think about that overbearing brute, not one bit because Amelia Dunbar was a rational woman, an independent woman. She would never let a man distract her from her... *"Bloody hell!"* Amelia cursed when she looked down and saw the dried herbs floating in the pitcher of milk instead of going into the pouches.

Amelia was muttering under her breath, cleaning up the mess, when a knock came at the door. She opened it to find one of the MacGregor warriors standing outside looking somewhat perturbed. He was a stocky man with a full head of red hair and a bushy beard.

"Scuse me, miss. I heard you are the healer?"

"Tis true. Do you have something that ails you?"

"Aye." He blushed. "The name's Rory," — he reached out to shake her hand — "I need your advice on... ah... a sensitive matter."

"Well, come on in then, Rory."

After some coaxing from Amelia and a lot of blushing from Rory, he finally admitted to having chafed inner thighs.

"Is that all Rory? The way you go on, I thought your man-part was about to fall off." Amelia rolled her eyes, and Rory immediately relaxed and chuckled.

Amelia prepared a balm to soothe the skin. Rory also drank some of her herbal tea to ease the joint pain he complained about. When Rory left, he felt refreshed, and his thighs were far less chafed.

Fifteen minutes later, there was another knock at the door. When Amelia opened it, there was a line of MacGregor retainers needing treatment for several ailments.

Amelia rolled up her sleeves, prepared some cool cider for those waiting outside, then she treated them one by one. The last of her patients was sitting at her table, Lachlan. She was applying a poultice containing comfrey to a burn on his arm.

"Do you have a healer at MacGregor Keep?" Amelia asked.

Lachlan shuddered. "Aye, we do, but it scares most of us to see her."

"Why?" Amelia continued wrapping the poultice and tied it off.

"They call her Morag, the witch. She has white eyes and has the sight."

"Come now Lachlan, you ken they call me a witch too because of my strange eyes." Amelia rebuked him as she cleaned her hands of the comfrey paste.

"Och, but you have proven to all of us you are not a witch."

"How so?"

"Well, the way you were pointing your broom at the Kennedy laird yesterday, if you were a witch, he would have turned into a toad right there on the spot."

Amelia stared at Lachlan, who was grinning at her, and she burst out laughing.

It had been such a long time since Amelia enjoyed a merry laugh. She accidentally snorted, then blushed, then snorted again and froze, placing a hand across her nose. The look on her face caused Lachlan to burst out laughing, and before long, they were both clutching their bellies in mirth.

It was then the door to the cottage flung open, almost splintering from the hinges. Beiste stood in the doorway, glaring daggers at Lachlan like a looming black shadow. "What is going on in here?" he growled.

Lachlan immediately sobered. "Miss Amelia is seeing to my burn."

Amelia wiped the tears from her eyes, still chuckling.

"Then what were you laughing about?" Beiste snapped.

"Lachlan said, if I was a witch, the Kennedy laird should have turned into a toad yesterday," Amelia replied while giggling.

Gads, she looked so bonnie when she laughed was all Beiste could think about as he drank in the sight of her, every inch. She was lovely. It rankled him that Lachlan and most of his men had spent time with Amelia. When they returned to camp, it was all they talked about, how gentle her touch was, how funny she was, how clever she was, how bonnie she was. Beiste wanted to punch each one of them in the face. And now Lachlan made Amelia laugh. Something Beiste wished he could do.

"If your treatment is done, leave!"

Lachlan immediately stood, but not before Amelia told him to wait. She moved to the mantle and handed him a jar.

"Keep the bandage dry for two days, then clean and dry the wound and use this balm."

"Thank you." Lachlan smiled at her, then left the cottage.

Amelia sat down again and suddenly felt aware of Beiste. She could feel his gaze on her as if they were physically touching. He remained standing.

"Would you like to sit down?" Amelia gestured to a spare chair.

"Aye." Beiste sat then said nothing more.

Amelia asked, "How are things with Mary?"

"Who?"

"Mary, your betrothed."

"Good."

More silence.

"Would you like some cider or something to eat?" Amelia asked.

"Aye, cider."

Beiste did not know why he was sitting in this cottage, but for the life of him, he did not want to be anywhere else.

Amelia poured cool cider into a cup. Her hand brushed against his when she handed it to him, and it felt like an angel touched his fingers.

Beiste said, "I thank you for seeing to my men. I will ensure you receive coin for your time."

"There's no need. They have offered to repair a few things around the cottage for me, which would be sufficient payment," Amelia replied.

"No! They will not have time to be hanging about your cottage." Beiste did not want any man enjoying her smiles and cider without him.

More awkward silence.

Beiste looked around, taking in the room. It struck him by how clean it was, and the scent of fresh flowers and herbs was calming. Her windows were open, letting the fresh air in and there were touches of color about the room from patterns in the wool blankets and colorful plants. It was tidy, practical, homely. There was nothing but warmth inside. A testament to the occupant within.

"How long have you lived here?" he asked.

"Since I was born. Twas my ma's cottage."

"Where is she now?"

"She died when I was fifteen."

"I'm sorry."

Silence again.

"What of your family?" Amelia asked, to fill the tense void.

Beiste drank some cider, then responded, "My da has passed, mercenaries killed him."

Amelia gasped. "I am sorry to hear it."

She said no more, not knowing what else to say when Beiste said, "Ma did not cope well after his death. Twas like her mind snapped with grief. She becomes confused easily, you ken?"

"I do. It must be difficult for her and you."

"Aye, she used to be so strong, like a warrior, and overnight, tis like she became a ghost. I have a *piuthar* as well. Her name is Sorcha."

"How old is she?"

Beiste smiled when he spoke of his sister. "She is fifteen, going on twenty." He laughed, then caught himself. Amelia was smiling at him, and he sobered. "Sorcha has an affliction."

This had Amelia sitting up with curiosity.

"She cannot talk. The morning they killed my da, Sorcha lost her voice and never spoke again."

"That is strange."

"A physician said something in her mind was broken."

Amelia just nodded.

Then Beiste asked, "Have you heard of such a thing?"

"No, but I ken the mind is powerful, and mayhap in time we will ken more about the way it works."

Beiste studied Amelia, and it surprised him how easy it was to talk to her when she was not screeching about something. She was wise, and she was kind. He did not understand why he shared about his family, but he had to admit he felt better for it.

He looked about the cottage again and saw jars of purple paste. "What is that for?"

"Tis an ointment to help with knee pain."

"Ah, I see."

"Actually," Amelia paused for a moment, "I hope you dinnae mind me being forward, but I prepared something for you. I was not sure whether you'd welcome it."

"Depends. What is it?"

Amelia walked to her workbench and pulled out a small jar, handing it to Beiste.

"Tis a salve to help soothe your scar. I have used it on scars before and it helps to ease the tightness of the skin."

Beiste just gazed at her. It touched him that she would think of helping him. He cleared this throat and muttered, "Thank you. I will try it."

More silence.

"Do you have any other ailment you wish me to remedy?" Amelia asked, wondering if maybe that was the real reason he was there.

Beiste knew the ailment he suffered from could only be remedied if he was deep inside her, but he was not about to tell her that. *Blast.* He needed to stop these lustful thoughts.

Amelia's body felt hot and flustered the more Beiste stared at her. Her breathing became shallow. A faint blush ran from her cleavage to her neck.

Beiste leisurely followed her blush with his gaze and looked back up at her lips as he focused on the softness of them. Then he cleared his throat. "I, uh, do have a slight pain in my... hand."

Eager to have something to focus on, Amelia instantly stood and crossed to the other side of the table, sitting beside Beiste. "Well, let me see what I can do for you."

She lifted his left hand and studied it profusely before Beiste said, "Uh, not that hand, this one." He extended his right hand out to her.

"Sorry. I should have asked which one it was first." She blushed with embarrassment. Then she took his hand in both of hers and examined it with extreme focus. Truth be told, Amelia could see nothing wrong with it, but she did not want to look silly a second time.

Beiste knew there was nothing wrong with his hand. He just wanted Amelia closer and touching him. He thought it was a superb idea, but now he was in hell. Pure hell, no stopping at purgatory, just go straight to hell. He was there because having her this close and being able to smell her lilac scent and gaze down at the top of her ample breasts and those luscious lips while she gently caressed his hand caused him to suffer from a severe case of blue balls.

Beiste had visions of her naked and straddling his lap, riding his length until he came. The thought alone worsened his predicament. He could not adjust his trews, or she would see the obvious evidence of his reaction to her, and he could not stand and leave without causing himself pain, so he was trapped in a pit of burning hell. Beiste gritted his teeth. Either he pushed her away or rolled himself out the door.

"I cannot see anything wrong with your hand," Amelia said. She looked up, puzzled, and locked eyes with him. Immediately, he knew she was not unaffected by him, either. Beiste heard her sudden intake of breath, and a blush covered her cheeks. It was as if time was suspended again, and it was only the two of them alone in the world.

Beiste needed to know what she tasted like, what it would be like to sup from her lips, just one taste, then maybe this maddening obsession would end. He leaned his head closer towards hers. Amelia still held Beiste's hand. She moved, closing the distance between them. Her lips parted, her tongue darted out to moisten her bottom lip and Beiste was undone. He was so close now, his lips almost brushing hers.

'Bang bang bang' came the knock at the door.

Blast, not now!

Amelia instantly pulled away as if coming to her senses.

No, come back! Beiste wanted to kill whoever was on the other side of that door.

Amelia was shocked at her wanton behavior. She stood and straightened her tunic. "Come in," she yelled.

Beiste felt the separation immediately. He wanted to grab her hand again, but knew he needed to gain control. As the haze cleared, he wondered what the hell he was thinking.

The door opened, admitting Brodie.

Brodie stood in the doorway, slightly surprised to see Beiste in the cottage. Brodie looked at Amelia, then back at Beiste, then back at Amelia. Then he smiled and stretched his arms out wide.

"Well, if it isn't my two most favorite people in the whole world!" Brodie declared.

"He... hello Brodie," Amelia stammered before Brodie wrapped her in a bear hug.

Beiste was on his feet, fists clenched on both sides, and he snarled. "What the devil are you doing here, Brodie?"

Brodie released Amelia and asked, "Brother, why so tense?" Brodie then plonked himself on a chair and addressed Amelia. "I have a message from the Castle for you. Lady Agnes and Lady Mary," — Brodie turned to Beiste — "*your* betrothed in case you may have forgotten," — he turned back to Amelia — "would like to see you. They say tis of great importance."

"Thank you," Amelia replied. "I'll head up there now."

Brodie nodded, then glowered at Beiste. "Brother, I think it best we make our way back to camp." The tone he used brooked no opposition.

✦

ON THE WAY TO THEIR campsite, Beiste was quiet, waiting for Brodie to launch into one of his rare speeches.

"Word of advice, Brother. You need to focus on your betrothed, for all our sakes."

Beiste just gritted his teeth but said nothing.

Brodie took that as his cue to continue. "We have been here two days, and you have spent more time chasing after the bonnie, wee, healer instead of Lady Mary. We all like Amelia. She's a good lass, but for the sake of our clan, you need to focus on your duty."

There was that word again: *duty*. Beiste agreed. Brodie was right. Beiste would be a fool if he let his obsession impede an oath to a king. Beiste replied, "I hear you, Brother." He then resolved to let Amelia go.

The Earl's Study, Dunbar Castle

AMELIA MADE HER WAY to her father's study, where Mary and Lady Agnes were waiting for her. Mary came running over to her straight away. She was in tears.

"Da says there is nothing he can do to break the betrothal." Mary sobbed. "He gathered the councilmen to look over the parchments and they all agree tis iron clad."

Amelia instantly hugged Mary and looked at her *seanmhair* for confirmation. Lady Agnes nodded, and the Earl looked resigned.

"I will only marry for love. I will only marry for love," Mary kept repeating.

The mood was sombre, and Amelia felt only sadness, not just for Mary but for herself, and she knew not why.

Pre-Betrothal Dinner

THAT NIGHT IN THE GREAT Hall, Beiste and the MacGregor War Band gathered for the pre-betrothal dinner with the Dunbars. The noble families and dignitaries sat on the dais while Amelia sat with the rest of the villagers at the trestle tables.

It was the first time Amelia had seen Beiste since their moment in the cottage. She was happy to see him. He was to become her brother-in-law, after all. Amelia was about to greet him but refrained when Beiste gave her a look of utter contempt as if she were vermin. Then his eyes cut right through her like she did not exist.

She understood. He was reminding her of her place. It still stung to be reminded so often. Amelia felt the rejection acutely and spent the rest of the night refusing to look at the dais again.

Throughout the meal, some MacGregor retainers she had treated came over to talk and spin yarns. Before long she laughed at their tales. But soon other village folk ventured forth to join in the ribaldry, and they nudged her out of the circle.

As Amelia observed the surrounding festivities, she realized for the first time how utterly alone she was. In a hall full of people, she sat on the periphery an outsider looking in. That thought provoked her more than any other thought in the past seven years.

EARLY THE NEXT DAY Amelia left her cottage before sunrise, avoiding any MacGregor retainers and especially their chieftain. She needed to escape to the one place she always felt at peace, the one place she belonged.

Wearing a long green hooded cloak, trews, and tunic she took a basket packed with necessary provisions, a hunting knife, and a small spade for foraging. Amelia made up her mind to forgo the betrothal festivities and spend the next few days deep in the woods by the river where she could forage for more herbs and wild vegetables.

It was time she started planning her own future, time she kept a promise to her ma. With that resolve she walked deep into the forest, unaware of the trouble that was brewing on the home front.

Chapter 7

Council Room, Dunbar Castle

Runaway

It was the morning of the betrothal ceremony and often on such auspicious occasions as these, it would help to have both parties to the agreement present. Unfortunately, on this day, one party had disappeared. The entire castle was in a frenzy.

Beiste stood with his arms folded, staring down at the Earl and his councillors. "What do you mean, Mary has run away?"

The Earl spoke up, his voice hoarse, his demeanor serious, contemplative, his hair disheveled. "Mary has run off to *Gretna Green* during the night with a Patrick Fraser."

Beiste gritted his teeth. This was not going as he planned. He had just resolved to marry the chit and, by the gods, someone better pay for this blunder.

Brodie addressed the room, the jovial man now replaced by an angry bear. "You realize this is a slight to the MacGregors and the King? We have every right to seek damages for a broken contract or wage war!" He banged his fist on the table.

The Earl paled. "Aye, I ken it." Maldred looked as if he had aged twenty years since the night before.

Beiste signaled to two retainers and said, "See if you can track them." They nodded and quit the room. He then said, "I suggest we wait until we receive word of Mary's whereabouts, and then we plan from there."

The Earl and the councilmen agreed.

Late in the evening, trackers returned with news for the castle. It did not bode well. Mary was well and truly wed to Laird Patrick Fraser, and he sent word that he would not relinquish his bride ever.

No betrothal ceremony took place that night. No festival banquet took place that night. Instead, a group of men sat around a gigantic table and debated the problem at hand.

Both parties were liable to the king if an alternative was not found within three days.

By morning, they were no closer to reaching a consensus on what they should do.

Meanwhile, in an inn beyond *Gretna Green*, Mary and Patrick Fraser, who bonded over berry tarts and Market Days, married for love.

Balm

THE FOLLOWING DAY, the mood on the estate was sombre. News spread of Mary's ruin and to the noble gentry among them, running off to marry for love was deemed scandalous. However, to many of the common folk and romantics at heart, the fact Mary had caught the eye of a handsome laird from a favorable clan lessened the outrage somewhat.

But for Beiste, he spent a restless night, not only having been jilted by his betrothed so publicly, but because he was feeling out of sorts. Maybe one of his *humours* was out of alignment. He wondered not for the first time if it was best to return to MacGregor Keep and send a missive to King MacBeth informing him of what had happened.

There was no way Beiste was waging war on the Frasers, which was what the council had recommended. If they wanted restitution, then they could bloody well send their own men into battle over some reckless girl. Also, the thought of leaving *Dunbar* troubled him somehow. Even though he knew it had to do with the healer, he knew it wouldn't come to anything. He made sure of it the night he cut Amelia to the quick. He had hurt her, but she masked it quickly.

Beiste was interrupted from his thoughts when Lachlan approached him, asking if he had seen Amelia.

"Why are you needing to see her?" he asked.

"I just wanted some more of that balm she gave me. But the cottage is all locked up, and no one has seen her for a while."

"What do you mean, no one has seen her?" Beiste was already worrying.

"Some women folk needed herbs and there were villagers wanting salves for their bairns and they were all down there complaining because Amelia was not there yestereve either."

"Has anyone gone in search of her to see if she's safe at least?"

Lachlan just shrugged.

Beiste headed to the castle. Amelia was missing, and he didn't like it. He would not rest until someone had some knowledge of her whereabouts. He never questioned why he was more concerned about Amelia's disappearance rather than Mary's.

Riverside

THE RIVER WAS FLOWING; the birds were tweeting; the sunlight broke through the early morning dew melting the frigid air. Amelia had been in the forest for the past two days. She knew Mary was betrothed by now and would already be on her way to the Highlands. Amelia would miss seeing her sister, but she could do without seeing that behemoth. A part of her thought to request that she travel with them to the Highlands but explaining the why of it and having to journey with a chieftain who did not want her around would be awkward.

No, she would stay in the forest a few more days, build up her supplies and sell them at the market for coin, then pay her own way. Besides, it was tranquil; it was peaceful. No one bothered her out here and no one could make her feel unwanted.

She had bathed in the river that morning and eaten a breakfast of fresh berries, plants, and nuts she had foraged from the forest. She had forgotten how restful it was out here in nature, without the constant chores and interruptions of the healer's cottage and the constant demands of the estate and her own family.

Amelia realized for the first time that she had spent seven long years caring for everyone else, but who cared for her? Who cared whether she lived or died? *No one.* It was a sobering thought. She had kin who knew nothing of her and a family who acknowledged her only as a *companion*. Amelia knew it was time to set her path. The rest of the world be damned.

Brodie

BRODIE WAS MAKING HIS way back to Dunbar Castle, having spent a few pleasurable hours shacked up with a saucy widow from the local village. Flora was her name or *Fiona?* He could not recall. He was not good with names. What he remembered with clarity was a story the widow imparted regarding the Earl of Dunbar and his not one but *two* lovely daughters.

It would appear old Maldred had not offered full disclosure of his offspring. It was something Brodie could push to their advantage, and if all went according to plan, his chieftain may still satisfy the betrothal contracts after all.

Having reached the castle, Brodie found Beiste and said, "I think I may have a solution to your problem. Turns out the Earl has *two* daughters of marriageable age. They are half-sisters."

Beiste did not like having to go through the entire process with another unknown woman. He was hesitant to pursue things further, however, the security of their lands was now at stake.

"All right then, who is this other wench?" he asked.

"Why, my dear Brother, she is none other than the bonnie healer you cannot stop obsessing about."

Beiste looked at Brodie in disbelief. "You dinnae say?"

Brodie raised his eyebrows in agreement. "Aye, Amelia is Maldred's daughter by a leman. She is older than Mary. The gossip is he was in love with Amelia's *màthair,* but he was betrothed since birth to Mary's."

Beiste was getting angry now. "So, he kept one in the village and one in the castle. But wouldn't her illegitimacy weaken the contract?"

"Well now, that's where you're wrong. The Earl had secret legal papers drawn up, acknowledging Amelia as his issue with a dowry and some rights of inheritance."

"Then why did he not offer her as a solution when the council met?" Beiste asked.

"Tis something we will need to find out."

"By the way, Brodie, how did you learn of all this?" Beiste asked.

"A wee bit of pillow talk, with the lawyer's widow, never goes astray," Brodie smirked.

Beiste just shook his head and said, "Someday Brodie Fletcher, you will fall for a woman who will be immune to your charms."

Brodie scoffed. "Och, is she breathing? I highly doubt it."

Ultimatum

BEISTE STORMED INTO the council room and said, "The betrothal can go ahead. The parchment states you are to provide a daughter in marriage to the MacGregor by the end of the sennight."

"But Mary has gone." Maldred looked puzzled.

"Mary has gone, but you have another daughter. The decree says I have to marry your daughter. It does not say which one."

"No! You cannot mean Amelia?" Maldred looked distressed. He started pacing.

"I do."

"Absolutely not! I promised her *màthair* I would do well by her. Besides, she is illegitimate any claim would not be legal." Maldred capitulated.

"But you acknowledge her, Maldred. She holds the same rights as a legitimate child." Lady Agnes had quietly walked into the room, interrupting the conversation.

"*Màthair,* stay out of this!" Maldred yelled.

"I also promised Amelia's *màthair* I would take care of her, but what have we done, son? We have kept her here when she has yearned to travel afar," Lady Agnes replied.

"*Mamaidh,* this is not the time."

"Then when, Maldred? You need to stop doing all in your power to keep her chained here."

"What do you mean? I have done everything for Amelia, even tried to find her a suitable marriage. It is she who keeps refusing," Maldred replied with annoyance.

Lady Agnes raised her eyebrow and asked, "Really, son? Why have all the men you chose for her been ones you kenned she would refuse?"

Maldred was red-faced, looking guilty. "But I need Amelia. She is the only one who kens how to handle the crofters, the only one who can heal the farmers and the womenfolk and the bairns. Even the tenants go to her when they need help because she is the only one who kens what to do. I cannot let her leave, I will not."

It made sense to Beiste why in an estate this large, the one person everyone relied on was Amelia.

Beiste said, "Then I suggest tis high time you handled your own affairs from now on because when I leave here in the morning, Amelia will come with me."

"No, please, she is my only connection to her *màthair*," Maldred pleaded.

"Tis done! Amelia is mine. If you deny me, there will be war," Beiste replied.

Maldred sat down and slumped in his seat, resigned to his fate.

Brodie interrupted them both when he said, "Well, I am glad we are all in agreement. Now, that brings us to the next question. Where on earth is Amelia?"

TEN MINUTES LATER, the room was full of men arguing and shouting. Well, mainly Beiste shouting after he had pieced together where his betrothed could be. It would appear she always went on her own with no escort into the forest. Amelia could disappear for days at a time, and no one would know her whereabouts.

"Earl, you realize your land borders the Marches? Any wandering group of men from England or gods knows where could set upon her and no one would ken!" Beiste growled. He was furious that these people had such little concern for Amelia's safety. She took on all their cares and not a single sorry one of them returned the favor.

"You must understand, Amelia is an independent soul. She kens her way around the woods better than anyone. She has always been safe," Lady Agnes replied.

"All it takes is *one* time for things to go wrong. No woman on MacGregor land goes without an escort in these dangerous times. A rival clan could take a woman and force your hand," Brodie said.

Beiste was already signaling his men to move. "I will find her, and when I return, I want the betrothal contracts signed and necessary ceremony carried out straight away. I will not let any more time lapse on the agreement."

On their way out of the castle, Harold, a crofter, said he knew where Amelia usually went and gave them directions to the river. Beiste had visions of her lying dead somewhere or being attacked by wild animals or kidnapped by rival clans or, worse, set upon by mercenaries.

He mounted his destrier and with the War Band they moved out, following Harold's directions. And when Beiste found her, the first thing he was going to do was put a bloody guard on her every second of the day, maybe even three guards. He decided right there and then that no wife of his would hie off alone to the woods whenever she bloody well felt like it.

Retrieval

AMELIA HAD JUST FINISHED cooking small flat flour cakes and fish she had caught from the river. She had seasoned it with wild onions and fresh herbs. Few people ventured to this part of the river. It was secluded, and the rocky boulders provided a windbreak from the elements which kept her makeshift shelter of woven flax and wood, warm and dry during the cooler nights. It also provided privacy, so she was not exposed and could see anyone approaching from afar.

Amelia had her notes with her so she could record and scribe herbs and plants she came across. She was just sitting in the soft tall grass enjoying her simple fare when she heard a commotion nearby. Instantly rolling onto her stomach, she tried to get a better look.

It startled her to see men walking through the woodlands. She panicked. *What if they were raiders?* Then she heard Beiste's voice shout, "Amelia, we ken you're there, tis the MacGregors."

Why on earth were the MacGregors out in the woods? Had something happened to Mary?

Amelia stood up, staring at the group. "What has happened? Why are you all here?"

Beiste swore she looked like a woodland nymph. He had seen nothing lovelier than Amelia in the forest. Her hair was windswept and curly, her tunic blew in the breeze. She looked so relaxed and resplendent in the sunshine. She was beautiful, and she vibrated health and vitality. He had to admit it, and she was his. *Mine!* growled that possessive voice in his head.

"*Gad's*, is she wearing trews? The way they cling to her thighs, tis criminal," said Brodie.

Then Kieran piped in, "I have never seen pants look that good on a woman before."

"Me either," Rory replied.

Beiste noticed Lachlan was also staring at Amelia like a stunned cow in a paddock. Beiste looked around and noticed the admiration was not just from him but *all* his men, they were all smiling at her and casually waving their 'hellos' *the imbeciles*. He glared at all of them, then stomped towards his betrothed.

"What the devil are you wearing? You should not be wearing men's apparel!" He scowled.

At first, Amelia was shocked they were there, and then she was annoyed they had intruded on her quiet time in the forest, and then she was livid that the big brute marching towards her was doing so without a care for the tranquillity of the environment. *Poor Mary, having to put up with that for the rest of her life,* she thought.

"Cover yourself now," Beiste demanded, while standing in front of her.

"What are you talking about?" she snapped.

"Your trews. It shows my men everything and when I say everything, I mean *everything*."

"You came all the way out here to complain about my garments?"

"Aye. Tis scandalous!"

"No, what is scandalous is that you stomp your big arse over here making a ruckus about my trews," Amelia hissed. With that, she turned her curvaceous, trews clad bottom around and stormed back to her campsite.

Beiste just groaned.

By this time, some of his men had gathered around Amelia's fire and were looking around her makeshift camp.

"Lachlan, if you take another bite of my fish, so help me, I will clobber you." Amelia swiped the piece of fish out of his fingers before it could reach his lips.

"But tis so tasty. What herbs do ye use?"

"Aye, this bread is so soft, Lass. Is that rye flour?" Brodie asked, breaking a piece off and dipping it into her fish sauce left in the pan.

"What are ye all doing here, anyway?" she asked.

They all went quiet and looked at Beiste.

He seemed at a loss about how to broach the topic of their betrothal, so instead, he did what he knew was best for now; he stalled.

"Mary has run away, and the Earl needs you to return to the castle immediately," Beiste blurted out.

"What? When? Is she all right? Why didna you say so before you daft, man?"

Before Beiste could explain, Amelia was already scurrying around packing up her things and issuing orders to his men who it surprised Beiste to observe, obeyed without complaint.

By the time they set off, they each had seeds and herbal arrangements to carry. When it was time to leave, Beiste swung Amelia onto *Lucifer* before she could protest and commanded them all to ride.

THE DOOR BURST OPEN to Maldred's study, and it was Amelia.

"Da, have you sent anyone to find Mary yet? What has happened to her? Da, speak to me!"

"Calm lass, Mary has eloped with Patrick Fraser."

She looked around at Beiste and her father, who then explained what had happened.

"So, what will you all do now? The King will not be pleased with this news," Amelia said.

Her father cleared his throat. "Well, we may have an alternative."

"Which I'll announce tonight," Beiste replied.

Chapter 8

New Beginnings

Beiste watched as Amelia made her way into the Great Hall. She was about to sit below on the trestle tables when her father and grandmother ushered her forward to sit at the dais. Amelia looked beautiful, in a red ankle-length kirtle and a woolen shawl. She also looked somewhat confused.

He fixed his gaze on her and studied her some more. Beiste did not dare analyze the strange feeling of possessiveness that came over him whenever he thought about her. All he knew was she did not know her fate was sealed. He only hoped Amelia would not hate him for what was about to transpire.

As the hall filled, the crowds gathered, waiting for the announcement of a betrothal.

Maldred stood in all his finery to address his clan. "Good people of Dunbar, today tis my pleasure to announce the betrothal of my daughter to chieftain MacGregor."

Amelia looked around. *Had Mary returned? What was happening?* She looked at her *seanmhair,* Agnes, who just smiled.

Then a voice boomed across the Great Hall.

"I, Beiste MacGregor, chieftain of the MacGregors of *Glenorchy,* have signed and formalized the betrothal between myself and my future wife, Amelia Dunbar. *Nighean* of your good Earl, Maldred."

Amelia's face drained of all color. The villagers murmured in shock. Amelia could not believe her ears. *He could not be serious?* What on earth was happening?

Staring directly into Amelia's eyes, Beiste spoke the three words that would change their lives forever. "I... choose... you."

Amelia looked about the room as people stood and started cheering and clapping.

"Go on, lass, go stand with your betrothed." Lady Agnes ushered Amelia towards Beiste. Amelia walked towards him in a daze, still too stunned to process what was happening.

Beiste held out his hand to Amelia. She hesitated, then ambled towards him, placing her hand in his. Beiste clasped her hand and pulled her into his side. He wound one arm around her back. Amelia looked about the room and at his War Band, and then she stared at Beiste. Then, for the first time in her entire life, Amelia fainted.

Betrothed

WHEN AMELIA CAME TO, she was ensconced in muscular arms. She glanced up to see Beiste studying her with concern. She sat up and faced the crowd, feeling embarrassed. Amelia smiled at everyone and then they all calmed. Her father announced the festivities could begin.

Immediately the minstrels started playing music with lyre and lutes and drums and a procession of serving women from the kitchens brought out enormous silver platters filled with succulent roasted venison, partridge, and boar. There were also platters of bread and cheese and decadent pastries, fresh fruit and nuts.

Beiste could see Amelia wanted to talk, but he cut her off. "We will talk of this later. For now, you must smile and enjoy the festivities."

"I cannot marry you. You must understand, this is not what I want," Amelia pleaded.

Beiste was angry at her rejection. "You will marry me, tis already decided. I dinnae care what you want."

Frustrated, Amelia kicked Beiste hard in the shin under the table. Brodie, who sat on the other side of Amelia, chortled, so she kicked him, too. "Ouch, what did I do?" Brodie asked.

"That was for not giving me any warning in the forest." Amelia was seething. They all knew, and no one thought to tell her or warn her, not her *seanmhair*, or her *father* or her daft betrothed. They just decided her future without consulting her about any of it.

Amelia turned back to Beiste, intending to give him a stern talking to, but when she opened her mouth, Beiste stuffed some meat and cheese from his platter in it.

"Come now, Amie, you need to eat. I'm sure you must be famished after a big day," he said.

Amelia tasted the food and realized she was starving seeing as the big oaf had interrupted her breakfast and she had not eaten for hours. Never one to turn down tasty food in a crisis, she huffed and then kept chewing and ignored both the men sitting beside her.

She pulled Beiste's platter of food away from him, placing it in front of herself, and dug in with gusto. When Beiste tried to pick some fruit from the platter, Amelia slapped his hand away and glared at him.

Beiste wanted to laugh, but he was afraid she might stab him with her *sgian-dubh*. Amelia already had it out and was stabbing at some meat on her plate.

Brodie poured some cider and placed it in front of Amelia, then dashed his hand away when she snarled at him. Amelia took the cider and drank a little, then kept eating completely, ignoring both men.

Brodie and Beiste exchanged glances, and they tried hard to contain their mirth. Beiste had never met a woman like Amelia before. She really was not frightened of him or any of his men, and he found that appealing.

After the festivities were over, Beiste and Brodie moved away to talk to their men, most likely to escape her glowering.

Lady Agnes approached Amelia and sat beside her. She poured some ale into a cup and addressed Amelia. "Child, I am sorry we gave you no warning," she said.

Amelia just shrugged. She really did not know what to say anymore.

"Believe me, if there was any other way, we would have taken it, but with Mary's ruin, it left us with only one option."

"Then why do I feel like I am the one being punished for her actions?"

"Amelia, I hope someday you see this as a gift to create your own destiny," Lady Agnes replied.

"I dinnae ken how I can create my destiny, when it seems you have all mapped out my future for me."

"We women are always caught up in the decisions of men, but tis a wise woman, Amelia, who learns to see an opportunity to thrive in every situation."

"I cannot see how one can thrive married to that overbearing brute," Amelia scoffed.

"Och, you are so headstrong and stubborn, just like your ma."

"Tell me about her please, we rarely speak of her anymore," Amelia said.

Lady Agnes took a deep breath and recanted her tale. "When Iona came here, she was running away from something. She came with the storm, and it smote Maldred. He wanted her, but he betrothed to Ealdgyth, so he kept Iona as his leman. I tried to discourage it, but then you were born, and their bond grew stronger. When Ealdgyth arrived, everything changed."

"What of Ma's kin? Did they never come for her?"

"We didna ken of Iona's past nor of her kin, for she would not speak of it. I urge you *ban-ogha* to look to the future now and let nothing hold you back."

Amelia hugged her *seanmhair*. It was the first time in her entire life she had referred to her as her granddaughter. Amelia took this as their farewell.

Soon after, Maldred approached. "Lia, tis sorry I am for everything. I ken I have not been an exemplary da to you, but I hope this union will provide you a good future."

Amelia did not know what to say. She sat quietly and said nothing.

Maldred continued to speak. "You remind me so much of Iona. Her spirit lives in you. Tis hard for me to part with you, tis like bidding her farewell again."

Amelia looked up and saw her father for the first time. He was a shell of a man still mourning the loss of a love he could never have. They rarely talked over the years, only when he needed something done for the estate, did he seek her out, or if he was trying to marry her off but seeing as she would leave in the morning this was Amelia's opportunity to ask what she had always wanted to ask.

"Why did you never look for her kin?"

The Earl stopped and stared at her. "What do you mean?"

"My *màthair,* she must have had a family before she came here. Why did you not search for them?"

"Iona would not tell me anything. She refused to talk about her past, and so I did not ask."

"Without her kin, it was easier to make her your leman," Amelia snapped.

"Lia, no, tis not how it was. We loved each other, and I sacrificed everything for your ma."

"What exactly did you sacrifice? You had your title and your family and your leman. You gained everything and sacrificed nothing."

Maldred looked stricken at her words, and Amelia felt guilty for causing him any more pain.

"I am sorry Da. I did not mean it. We all have our paths to follow. I love you and I will miss you."

For the first time in her life, the Earl reached across and hugged Amelia. "I love you too, *mo nighean,* and I hope this marriage brings you peace."

No Escape

AMELIA FEIGNED TIREDNESS, stating she needed to go back to the cottage. Beiste sent Kieran and Rory with her. Amelia calmly hiked her dress above her ankles and bolted towards the cottage. She knew she would need to make her escape now, or she would be chained to one mountain of an arrogant ox for the rest of her life.

Beiste knew Amelia was up to something. She had gone quiet. After she had eaten and seemed more relaxed, she had agreed to all his commands, almost demurely. He knew there was no way she would be that calm unless she had a plan.

Amelia hustled about the cottage, packing her bare provisions and belongings, and climbed out her back window. She had just landed on the ground with a thud when she heard Beiste's voice behind her. "Where do you think you're going, minx?"

She turned to see his arms folded, legs crossed, leaning on the back wall of her cottage just waiting for her. *Damn, the man was far too astute for his own good!*

Amelia picked up her sack and casually replied, "Where I go tis none of your concern. I have plans for my life and I willna let you ruin it." She was desperate. She needed to go find her mother's kin. She needed freedom, and she needed it now.

"And what plans might they be? The law requires you to obey me," Beiste said.

"Damn your laws! I dinnae want to be shackled to a man because of some stupid law."

Beiste snatched her sack from her. "Amelia, I am not just any man. I am a chieftain with land and wealth, and I offer you an honorable position as my wife, as the *màthair* of my heirs and the mistress of my clan."

The earnestness of Beiste's comment caused Amelia to pause and think about the wisdom of his words. And then he had to go and ruin it.

Beiste paused and with a bored expression said, "Trust me, Amelia, this is one of the best offers you'll get, for no man would abide your harsh tongue." Beiste immediately regretted his words when he saw the flicker of hurt flash across Amelia's face. But he was annoyed by her constant rejection.

"You are such a stupid brute! If it is a wife and heirs you want, I'm sure there are many women willing to spread their legs to oblige you if you only took time to work on your manners."

Beiste grimaced at her words. Amelia was right; he was being a brute, but enough was enough. His patience was at an end. She was his, and they were bound.

He began pacing towards her, like a predator stalking its prey. Amelia started backing away from him. As his eyes raked her body, Beiste's voice deepened into an inaudible whisper. "Let me assure you, Amie, there is only one woman I want spreading her legs beneath me to beget my heirs, and that woman is you. You... are... mine!"

Amelia blushed crimson red from the shocking imagery. She took another step back, only to come up hard against the wall. She was trapped. Beiste's words had flustered her, stirring strange feelings within. She felt hot and breathless and angry. How could this infuriating man have such a strange effect on her? Beiste was standing far too close now. She could not think with all that virile masculinity towering over her.

Before she could utter another protest, Beiste pulled Amelia into his arms and as his mouth came crashing down on hers, all rational thought scattered to the four winds.

Beiste did not know what came over him. All he knew was he had to kiss Amelia's sweet lips. The more she challenged, the more the predator within came to the fore. He was a beast, and she was like a siren calling sailors to their wreck and ruin. Something snapped at the thought she would reject him again. The moment his lips touched hers, Beiste knew he was gone.

He had been with women before, but nothing, none of them compared to this sweet, delectable vixen and temptress in his arms. Beiste closed his eyes, and his mind was filled with thoughts of her. He shuddered as he became aroused; it was almost painful. No woman had made him feel this level of passion before. From Amelia's tentative response, he knew she was innocent and yet there lay a dormant passion within, ready to burst forth.

Beiste coaxed her lips apart so he could taste her with his tongue, gently encouraging her, guiding her until he felt her respond. *Pure bliss.* If he felt this much from only a kiss, how much more would it feel to be inside her and have her writhing beneath him as he pumped his essence into her body?

Beiste's hands explored her luscious body, surprised by the abundant breasts and curvaceous bottom concealed by her attire. When they returned to his Keep, he would burn that dress as a sacrifice to the gods of plain apparel and he would make sure she wore nothing but finery to enhance her assets. As he deepened the kiss, he heard Amelia moan. He knew she was just as affected by their embrace. He felt her arms around his neck, pulling him closer as Amelia moved to deepen the kiss. Beiste knew he was losing control.

He had to stop. It would not do to have her overrun his senses. He was a seasoned warrior. There was no place for uncontrolled action. On that thought, Beiste tore his lips away from hers.

Amelia's eyes were closed, her lips glistening, and she looked dazed. He steadied her, then set her away from him. All he wanted was to pull her back into his arms and do more than kiss her, but not now. Not here. Not yet.

Beiste heard footsteps behind him, a reminder they were not alone.

He stepped away from Amelia, caught his breath, and in a harsher voice than he had intended, he commanded, "Get back in that cottage and stay there. We leave in the morning."

Amelia looked startled by his change of tone, and she blushed at her wanton behavior.

Beiste moved to speak to Kieran, who had come round the back of the cottage. "We leave first thing in the morning. Dinnae let my betrothed out of your sight. Sleep across her doorway if you have to." With that, he stormed back towards his destrier with nary a look in her direction.

Amelia felt a slow dull ache in her chest at the loss of his presence as the two guardsmen, Kieran and Rory, flanked her on both sides.

"Mistress, please come with us." They ushered her back into her cottage, then stood vigil one at the door, the other outside the window. There would be no chance of escape now.

Farewell

THE NEXT MORNING, AMELIA awoke to find a long line of villagers, crofters, and farmers at her door. Some bid farewell, others sought treatment, having heard she would be leaving. Amelia got busy preparing for each person a package of remedies to see them through the winter. She also arranged for her livestock to be cared for by the neighbors and her garden to be tended. There were also two midwives she instructed and distributed bottles of herbal mixes to assist them in their work. Finally, Amelia readied herself and packed the last lot of seedlings and pots and pouches she would need to take with her to her new home.

Once everything was complete, Amelia had one more thing to retrieve, her mother's box. She had hidden it in a secret panel under the floor of her bedchamber.

Beiste and his men were ready to leave, but he was still waiting for his betrothed. By the time he made his way to her cottage, his guards told him she was inside gathering the last of her belongings. His men told him she had been treating people since dawn. They had helped her pack, but she wanted to be alone.

Beiste was furious that so many people sought her help when they knew she needed to leave. When he finally saw her, she looked exhausted, and it was still early in the morning.

"Amie, come, tis time to go, Love,"

She looked up, and he saw the shadows under her eyes. Beiste instantly wanted to take the exhaustion away and beat the entire village for tiring her before a lengthy journey. Amelia was his to protect and he would make sure people treated her better.

"Aye, I will be there shortly. I need to gather a few things," Amelia replied.

"Then I will help you," Beiste replied.

"No, tis fine, I can do it. I wish to say goodbye to my home one last time."

Beiste saw the sadness in her eyes and nodded. He stood in the open doorway and let her have her time. "We can always come back to visit in the future if you want?"

Amelia gave him a wistful smile and shook her head. "Once I leave, I dinnae plan on ever returning."

Beiste noticed she held an oak box with such reverence. Someday he would enquire what was in it, but not today.

Amelia gathered the rest of her things and looked around one last time at the place that had been her home for so many years. She remembered her mother's arms reaching out to her when she was a child and all the times she had found solace, warmth, and love inside that cottage. She bid farewell to the memories and her past.

With unshed tears glistening in her eyes, Amelia turned towards her future. Beiste stood in the doorway, reaching his hand out towards her. She took it and they walked out together to embrace the new day.

Chapter 9

Dunbar to Glenorchy

Amelia sat upon her horse, surrounded by Beiste and his men. They rode in tight formation, protecting her within. They had now been riding for several hours with only limited breaks along the way and as darkness was approaching, they would set up camp soon. There was no need for a cart since they had distributed her belongings among the men. Her book and box were strapped to her horse and wrapped in cloth.

It was a sennight's hard ride to their destination, and they set a relentless pace. Amelia felt the effects on her backside and her thighs, but she refused to show any sign of weakness, keeping pace with the men. She would not cause any delay.

Beiste had remained distant towards her since they left the cottage and scarcely spoke for most of their ride. His expressionless mask returned, and his eyes were cold and assessing every time he glanced at her. It did not bother Amelia because no matter how distant Beiste could be towards her; he was not callous. He still saw to her needs, made sure she rode protected, and now and then she noticed he would check to make sure she was safe.

At one time, the weather had become chilly and her cloak, although thick, was no match for the icy winds that cut her skin as she rode. Amelia gritted her teeth to endure it when they were called to a stop. Beiste rode back towards her and without a word he pulled out a thick woolen plaid, wrapped it around her, covering her head, and then they continued. She felt the warmth instantly. He yelled out orders like a tyrant and they set off again. She knew he commanded significant power. But as much as he scowled, Amelia still could not bring herself to fear him. He rode ahead, leaving her with the two retainers, Kieran and Lachlan, who flanked her constantly.

As if to make up for his chieftain's inattention, Brodie rode by her side more than anyone else to keep her company, and he lightened the mood with his tales of adventures. Brodie made a friendly traveling companion, and the time passed quickly in his company. Rory had also talked to her more, and there was a sparkle in his eye. The other warriors kept a discreet distance. It was true what they said about the MacGregors. They protected their womenfolk.

Having been free for so long to do her own thing and not having anyone care where she was, Amelia found it stifling to be constantly followed and guarded. But there was nothing else for it but to comply. At least they were mostly polite to her, even if some men were gruff.

If she were to find her kin, at least they headed in the right direction and with protection, so Amelia did not complain.

Beiste and his men wanted to be away from the lowlands as much as possible and even further away from the English border. They also wanted to be on safer terrain in the Highlands. Traveling on public roads always had its share of dangers. There were mercenaries and thieves and sometimes rival clan territories to move across. It was a foolish man who did not have a care for his surroundings and dallied too long in the open.

As night approached on the second day, Beiste called the troupe to a halt, ordering they set up camp and get a good sleep. He also knew Amelia was exhausted and did not want her falling off her horse. He had admired her fortitude and resilience. Not once did she complain. She kept pace with them and refused to burden anyone. He wondered what her upbringing was like to make her so independent.

Immediately, his men set into action, securing the area, gathering wood, and building a campsite. Amelia, stiff from the ride, was trying to dismount when she was gently lifted off her horse by large hands. She was surprised to find Beiste holding her just as he set her down.

"Th... thank you, Chieftain," she stammered as circulation slowly returned to her legs.

"Beiste, that's my name. You will use it."

Amelia nodded.

"Are you well?" he asked, concern marring his features.

"Aye, I am hale, thank you. I am just a bit sore." She smiled up at him tentatively and, for a moment, his mask of indifference slipped before it was restored.

"Good, we will camp here for the night." With that, Beiste released her and disappeared.

Once the campsite was established, Amelia sat on a fallen down tree log with Brodie. They partook of a light repast of oatcakes, stewed meat, and cider. Beiste was still nowhere to be seen, so Amelia settled around the fire in the company of the men.

"Mistress, is it true you saved Rory's pecker from falling off?" Kieran asked.

"It wasna my pecker, you oaf, twas me thighs," Rory scoffed.

"Dinnae lie Rory, we all ken your pecker was close to rotting with under-use," Brodie said while the men chuckled and snickered.

"Mayhap tis your pecker that is rotting from *over-use,* Brodie," Rory replied.

Brodie stood, ready to belt Rory.

Amelia quickly intervened. "Stop that now! Nobody's manhood is rotting off and if it was, I am sure I have a salve that can help clear it up."

"Manhood? What is that?" Fergus raised his eyebrow.

"Manhood, tis the more genteel term for... your..." Amelia gestured towards his groin area.

"I dinnae ken what you mean," Rory said with a serious face.

"Come to think of it, neither do I. What exactly is a 'manhood'?" Brodie smirked.

Kieran scratched his beard. "I too dinnae understand what you mean by this term, Mistress."

"A manhood is your man-part." Amelia was getting flustered but kept pointing around the groin again.

"Och, you mean thigh?" Lachlan asked.

"No, I mean the thing you were talking about before." Amelia glared at Rory.

"No need to get impatient, Mistress, tis not our fault we dinnae ken your healer terms," Fergus said.

"Mayhap she means stomach, for we all ken the stomach is the way to a man's part," Brodie said, trying hard to keep a straight face.

"No, a 'manhood' is your pecker, the thing above your baw sack, your penis!" Amelia blurted out, exasperated.

The men made loud gasping noises, as if shocked.

"Well, now, Mistress, there's no need for you to get so vulgar." Kieran feigned disgust.

"Aye, tis inappropriate to discuss a penis in polite company," Brodie snorted.

Amelia blushed, but when she caught the sparkle in their eyes, she knew they had just been jesting with her.

"Bloody morons!" she shouted.

With that, they all roared with laughter. It was not too much longer before Amelia saw the humor in it too and giggled. Then she laughed so loud she inadvertently snorted. She covered her face in mortification and they all burst into hysterics at her expense.

A rustling came from behind them as the men stifled their laughter despite the mirth avidly displayed in their eyes.

Amelia felt a shadow cast over her. Looking up, she beheld a glaring Beiste as she covered her mouth to muffle her giggle.

"Why are you ladies sitting around here coddling my betrothed? We have a long ride on the morrow and tis still much to do. Get on with you!" Beiste growled at his men.

"Aye, Chief," they replied as the group dispersed. Amelia could hear their chuckles echoing through the nearby woods. She watched them leave before returning her gaze to Beiste. By the look of his displeasure, she knew he was about to bark some orders at her.

"Amelia! I'll not have you flirting with my men. There are dangers aplenty on these roads. They need to be alert instead of entertaining you." With those parting words, he turned and stormed off to the other side of the campsite. Leaving an open-mouthed Amelia in stunned silence. *What an ass.*

Beiste stormed into the clearing to gather his thoughts. He was furious at his men, engaging his betrothed in such ribaldry. He had done all he could to ignore her most of the day, only because she jumbled his thoughts and set his body on fire. If he spent too much time with her, he would likely consummate their union on the road, and there was no way he would do that within earshot of his men. He would do right by her, and their first time together would be in his bed, in his Keep, within the sanctity of marriage.

When he helped her dismount earlier, it took all his willpower to step away and not carry her into the woods and ravish her. To see her laughing with his men and enjoying the company of Brodie and Lachlan, the handsome louts, it just grated his insides. Beiste was never the jealous type until now. If only he could get her to laugh with him. But that would require him spending more time with her and with the direction his carnal thoughts were going, it would be a long trip home.

Sleeping Arrangements

WHEN THE MEN RETURNED from their chores, Kieran and Rory accompanied Amelia to a small stream to freshen up whilst they stood guard a few meters away.

Amelia stripped down to her chemise and, with a wet cloth and some soap, washed away as much of the dust and grime as she could. She had not seen Beiste again since mealtime and wondered where she would sleep. Pondering such thoughts, she scrubbed herself some more.

When Beiste returned to the campsite, he was clean, having taken a quick wash further downstream. The icy water rejuvenated his spirits. It was a habit for him and his men to wash when they could. He could not understand how some noblemen could go for days without bathing. It seemed barbaric to him. Beiste wondered about their sleeping arrangements for the night.

"Has Amelia returned?" he asked Brodie who was sitting by the campfire drinking cider.

"She is still by the stream."

Beiste nodded and made his way to her when he came upon Kieran and Rory, talking quietly with their backs to the stream.

"Chief, we need to ken whether you need her to sleep near us or whether—"

"She sleeps with me. You are both relieved."

Both men grinned and quietly left.

"Kieran? Rory? Are you still there?" Amelia yelled.

"Amie tis Beiste. I've come to escort you back to camp," Beiste replied.

Amelia stepped out from the bushes looking fresh and clean, wearing a kirtle and cloak. Beiste closed his eyes and drank in the scent of her. It felt erotic. He needed to get a grip on this or at least seek relief soon. He really had been far too long without a woman. That was it, he thought. It was not the effect of Amelia at all. He just had not been with a woman in such a long time. Maybe once he did, he would get her out of his system. Eventually, the feelings would wane. *Isn't that what happened to all marriages?*

"I'm ready." Amelia broke his train of thought and was standing before him with her overlong damp hair loose about her and that intoxicating fragrance.

Lilacs. She smelled of lilacs. Beiste gritted his teeth, her enticing scent playing havoc with his senses. "Good. Then we best be away," he said in a hoarse voice.

Beiste clasped Amelia by the hand and it felt like lightning shot through his body just from her touch.

Amelia thought she would faint when Beiste took her hand. It was like fire branding her. When they returned to the campsite, she released his hand and moved towards her belongings she had left in a corner of their make-shift shelter. She spread out her blanket and prepared her bedding.

"What do you think you are doing?" Beiste asked as he towered over her.

"I'm setting up my pallet to sleep," Amelia replied, frowning in confusion.

"Well, there does not seem to be enough room for me," Beiste grumbled.

"There isn't supposed to be room for you. I'm sleeping here alone."

"Not likely *mo chridhe.*"

"Beiste, I am fine sleeping alone." Amelia made to settle onto her pallet but instead found herself thrown over Beiste's shoulder as he moved her towards his pallet by the fire.

"Put me down!" she demanded.

He smacked her on the backside. "Shh, you'll wake the men." He smirked. Then gently laid her down on his pallet and joined her, wrapping his plaid around them both.

Amelia was fuming. "Why must you be so overbearing all the time?" She tried to move away from him, but Beiste reached out and pulled her body back, keeping her firmly tucked in place.

"Go to sleep wench, we have a long day of travel on the morrow." He tucked her head under his chin and settled into sleep.

Amelia was too tired to protest. The day's journey had taken its toll on her. She settled and enjoyed the smell of his clean, masculine scent. She had to admit he was very warm as she drifted off to sleep.

Rose Honey

FOR THE NEXT TWO DAYS, they set a relentless pace, but it was on the fifth day after they had passed Glasgow, four men set them upon. Beiste turned and his heart almost stopped at the sight of a dagger flying towards his betrothed. Amelia was too far away for him to intercept it.

Just before it hit her, he watched Kieran throw his body in front of Amelia and the dagger lodged in his shoulder; Kieran fell from his horse and Amelia screamed as she went down with him. Beiste was already galloping towards them. He shuddered to think what would have happened if Kieran had not been there.

Beiste thundered with rage as his sword cut down two men who had used that diversion to barrel down on Beiste. He watched as Brodie dispatched a third man with his axe. As another attacker tried to flee, Lachlan shot him with an arrow. He slumped forward.

They all dismounted and scanned the area for more men, but it seemed there were none.

Beiste roared with fury, running towards the attacker, who was writhing on the ground. "Who sent you?"

"Go to hell," the man replied.

Beiste hit him in the jaw, knocking him out. "Tie him up. He comes with us if he does not die beforehand. I want to ken who these men are and why they attacked us." Beiste was so full of rage he wanted to run the man through, but he needed to extract more information. He turned and kicked the man in the groin. "That's for trying to hurt my wife!"

Beiste moved to Amelia's side and knelt beside her. She was trying to stem the bleeding from Kieran's wound. Kieran was out cold from the fall. Beiste's men stood guard around her; swords ready for any further attack.

"Amelia, Love, are you all right?" Unable to help himself, Beiste pulled her head towards his and kissed her hard, then he murmured, "I could have lost you, *mo ghaol.*"

Amelia was startled by the kiss, but she reassured him, "I am fine, Beiste, truly."

They both gazed into each other's eyes, until the sound of someone clearing their throat broke their intimate moment.

"Scuse me, but I think I am the one who is dying and in need of some affection."

Amelia and Beiste both looked down and suddenly remembered Kieran was bleeding and lying in her lap.

"Oh, sorry Kieran, I will see to you straight away." Amelia quickly sprang into action and blushed that she had forgotten all about poor Kieran. Beiste moved away from her and started bellowing orders. He sent men to scout the area and ordered they stop for a rest break. This would give Amelia time to treat Kieran's injury.

Twenty minutes later, Amelia had her healing basket, and she had cleaned Kieran's wound. It was deep and in danger of becoming infected. She stitched his wound together as neatly as she could.

Kieran drank some whiskey to numb the pain; she had talked to him to distract him, but she noted he really was a big bairn. Amelia had witnessed nothing like it before, a gigantic man who kept saying, "Ow, ow, that hurts. Och, it will hurt, it will hurt." When she had not even touched him yet.

Once the ordeal was over, she worked on bandages for him, but she knew the exact thing which could assist with his healing was the one thing she did not have in her supplies. There had been a shortage of it at *Dunbar* that season.

Beiste came over to check on her. "How does he fare, Love?"

"Kieran is fine, he passed out from the pain so tis best he sleeps for a while."

"Is there anything you need?"

"A jar of rose honey would not go astray right now," Amelia replied in jest, knowing that she would just have to make do with a simple poultice in the meantime. She kept working on the strips of cloth.

Beiste stilled and stared at her, then he asked, "What did you just say?"

"I said a jar of rose-honey, tis scarce but very effective for healing and sealing wounds. There's something in the sticky part that protects the flesh from rotting and the rose petals have healing properties of their own."

Beiste just kept staring at her.

Amelia asked, "Is something the matter? You look like you've seen a ghost."

"Wait here," Beiste replied before he walked off. Within two minutes he was back at her side, having recovered the pouch and jar Morag had given him.

Amelia stared at the crushed rose petals and the jar of honey. "How on earth did you come by this?" she whispered in awe.

"Our clan healer, Morag, gave it to me. Before I left, she told me, *my wife* would ken what to do with it."

A shiver ran down Amelia's spine as they both stared at the items.

"But how did Morag ken you would marry me instead of Mary?"

Beiste just shrugged his shoulders.

"Well, thank you, Morag," Amelia whispered to the sky and began readying Kieran's bandages.

With Kieran's injury, they took a slower pace, but Beiste did not want to stop overnight again until they were in *Loch Lomond, Trossachs* region. He felt safer there knowing the terrain and they would be closer to *Glenorchy*. They could rest their horses then.

Several hours later, Amelia was struggling to remain on her horse. She was not used to this much riding ever. Every inch of her body ached. As they rode on, her eyes drooped with exhaustion. It was then she felt muscular arms enclose around her as she was lifted off her horse and transferred onto Beiste's lap. Beiste wrapped them both in his plaid and held her tight to his chest. "Sleep *mo leannan*," he gently commanded. Amelia rested her head against his chest and did just that.

Loch Lomond

IT WAS THE SEVENTH day on the road and at the slower pace, Amelia could appreciate the breath-taking view of the Highlands for the first time. She had thought the *North Coast Sea* and *River Tyne* around *Dunbar* to be serene until she set eyes on the glorious beauty of *Loch Lomond* and the mountains beyond. It was breath-taking and her soul sang with the feeling of being home. Amelia felt like she was walking in the footsteps of her ancestors. Her kin were somewhere here in the Highlands and her heart overflowed with excitement for the future ahead.

She was still riding with Beiste on *Lucifer* as he refused to let her return to her horse. But she was warm and did not care to argue.

Beiste could not understand why, but he needed to have Amelia close to him. It calmed him when he felt her soft against him. He had never felt this attached to a woman before, but he also did not fight it. He was looking forward to them setting up a proper campsite and resting a full night by the loch.

That night, they set up camp close to the water, sheltered by the trees. Amelia's ability to build her shelter, source food, and forage for plants impressed Beiste. She was a forest nymph. He also noticed she was comfortable around his men and even more comfortable around him. No matter how much he scowled, she just shrugged her shoulders.

The first night they arrived, they bathed in the loch and Amelia felt so fresh. Beiste found her and it almost unmanned him, watching her rise from the water, her chemise clinging to her curves. She resembled a sultry siren. Amelia had glimpsed Beiste, and she felt a sudden rush of heat when he stormed towards her and engaged in a passionate kiss. But he stopped just enough to get control.

"Come, Amie, we must eat and rest properly tonight, for tomorrow we will reach home."

They ate a tasty and abundant fare of fresh fish with herbs and spices he had never known could taste so good. Amelia also made them all flour, bread and oatcakes as they sat around the campfire.

That night, Beiste lay on his pallet and opened his plaid for Amelia to lie within. She came without hesitation now or argument. He liked that she sought him out and settled next to him with no awkwardness. Beiste slept well beside her and was restless if he awoke to find her gone. He could not understand how, in a scant time, he had become so used to her being with him. His body craved her nearness. They slept well.

The only thing that marred their stay was the next morning they discovered the man they had captured had escaped during the night and no one could fathom how. He had been secured with ropes, but by morning Fergus said he awoke to find him gone.

Beiste became extra vigilant of Amelia's safety. He did not like the thought that an attacker was on the loose. After their midday meal, they set off for the last leg of their journey.

It was time to go home.

Chapter 10

MacGregor Keep, Glenorchy, Scottish Highlands

Homecoming

Amelia had seen nothing as ethereal as MacGregor Keep. As their horses came over the rise, she had to catch her breath at the stunning view. The colossal stone structure was well situated beside a magnificent loch and, deep within her soul, she felt like she was finally home.

As they entered through the main gates and into the interior bailey, the area was filled with men, women, and children waving and cheering, providing a fitting welcome for their chieftain. Amelia noticed some friendly faces, and some eyed her with open suspicion. Amelia would not cower. She also observed several women ogling the men, especially her husband. She did not like that at all. Amelia instinctively moved further back into Beiste's embrace. Beiste, in return, tightened his arm around her.

Brodie even had women running alongside, vying for his attention. Some were trying to push others out of the way. But there was a woman who gave Amelia an openly hostile glare. She was pretty and tall with long blonde silken locks. She beamed at Beiste and waved, trying to garner his attention. Amelia knew that look and she did not like it. *How many women was she going to have to beat off with a stick?* She wondered.

Amelia felt a tingle on the back of her neck. She surveyed her surroundings and felt goose pimples across her skin. Someone was watching her, and she shuddered. She glimpsed a hooded figure in grey; it was a man; she could tell by his physique. He was staring directly at her, and she sensed pure hatred. Amelia clutched Beiste's arm, such was the fear he evoked.

Beiste stiffened behind her. "Are you all right?" he asked.

"Aye, tis just that man in the cloak."

Beiste was looking into the crowd. "What man do you speak of?"

Amelia looked around, but he had disappeared. "No one, no one, twas nothing," she replied.

Eventually, the horses stopped in front of steep steps which led into the Keep. Standing on the platform above was one of the most handsome men Amelia had ever seen. He wore a wolf's fur-lined coat with a leine underneath. He stood next to an older woman and a young lass.

Is that Beiste's brother? She wondered. There did not seem to be a family resemblance, although he looked serious. So, taken by his attire, Amelia kept staring when Beiste's arms tightened around her. His lips brushed against her ear, and he growled, 'That is Dalziel my second, and I'll ask you to stop undressing him with your eyes."

"I was not undressing him," Amelia snapped.

Beiste ignored her and was already dismounting the horse and reaching up to help her down. Amelia huffed. *Annoying man. Always jumping to conclusions.*

Beiste took a firm hold of her hand and walked up the steps, expecting her to follow. He stopped at Dalziel, shook his hand, and grunted, "This is Amelia. She is mine!" Then he turned to Amelia and said, "This is Dalziel. You will not be seeing much of him."

Amelia just stared wide eyed in shock at such rudeness.

Dalziel bowed his head slightly. "Welcome Mistress," he greeted with a smooth brogue. She caught a slight *Angles* accent.

Amelia smiled in return. "Thank you. I am so glad to meet you, Dalziel." She was extending her hand to shake his, but Beiste pulled her away before she could make contact.

"Come meet my *màthair* and Sorcha. We dinnae have time to gossip," he commanded.

Amelia gave Dalziel an apologetic smile when she caught him grinning at the ground. She could not believe the rudeness of the lummox dragging her about like a goat.

"Stop rushing me," she hissed in anger.

"Stop flirting," Beiste retorted. He knew he was being unreasonable, but he felt slightly wanting compared to the smooth-faced, handsome bastard Dalziel, who was smirking at him. *Asshole.* Why did he even keep him around? He should send him to the North.

"You are unbelievable!" the termagant beside him spat out. But he ignored her outburst and kept walking, dragging his reluctant betrothed in tow.

Soon, Amelia came face to face with Beiste's mother, Jonet. She knew straight away where Beiste inherited his features, for she was the same coloring as him. Bronzed complexion with long raven black hair.

Beiste gentled his voice when he spoke to his mother. "Ma, tis good to see you." He bent low and kissed her on the cheek. "I want you to meet my betrothed, Amelia."

Jonet stared at Amelia as if trying to remember something. Then she smiled and became so animated it even surprised Beiste. "Tis so good to see you again. I cannot believe it. You look so young. How are your brothers? Come, we must speak and catchup tis many a year I have not heard from you. Where have you been?" Jonet asked.

"Ma," Beiste said, "this is my Amelia. You have never met her before."

His mother looked confused. "Amelia? No, tis not her name, her name is... oh what is her name?" — Jonet kept flicking her fingers, trying to remember — "I cannot remember." She shook her head. "Why can't I remember your name when I ken you so well? What are your brothers' names again?"

"I have no brothers, Lady MacGregor," Amelia replied, gently taking Jonet's hand in hers. "I am a Dunbar and I have but one sister."

Beiste interjected, "She is a MacGregor now."

Amelia ignored him. "'Tis wonderful to meet you, Jonet."

Jonet clutched Amelia's hand, then her eyes cleared. "I'm sorry, lass. For a moment there, I thought you were someone else. Your eyes they are so familiar to me. I am easily confused these days." Jonet stared off into the distance in stony silence, but she did not release Amelia's hand. It was as if she found comfort in it.

Amelia looked at Beiste. His face was one of deep concern for his mother. When his eyes met Amelia's, she smiled back at him. It was a silent gesture that she understood. His eyes softened. He leaned across and kissed Amelia on the lips. Then gently took his mother's other hand. "Come, Ma, let us make our way to Sorcha."

Within minutes of meeting Sorcha, Amelia discovered two things. The first was that Sorcha had striking features like her brother and mother, but only fairer. She had long golden hair and deep blue eyes, which could mean she resembled her father. The second thing was, she was shy. A predicament that made her blush and stare at the ground a great deal. Amelia resolved to do her best to communicate with her new sister.

Sorcha came forward and hugged Beiste, and he kissed her hair. There was genuine affection between them and that gave Amelia more of an insight into her betrothed. Beiste was openly affectionate with his mother and sister and very protective.

Soon, their entourage made its way inside to the Great Hall as people followed beside them amidst a buzz of excitement. Amelia still felt dusty and road-worn. She longed to freshen up because she knew she must look a fright, but Beiste insisted he introduce her properly to the clan before they retire.

Once inside the Great Hall, Amelia was glad to observe it was clean with fresh rushes on the floor. The large, high wooden beams were intricately carved with heraldic designs. The raised dais was large enough to fit several nobles, and the table was laden with food and beverages. The minstrels were already playing softly, providing a fitting ambiance for an evening meal.

The main family made their way to the dais where Beiste seated Jonet and Sorcha; a woman in a long black outfit with stern features soon attended them. She looked to be only a little older than Amelia, and her name was Deidre. She served Jonet a warm tea and a grey-looking broth.

Beiste walked around to Amelia and together they remained standing. When the hall filled, he addressed his clan. "I present you to my betrothed, Amelia of Dunbar!" The crowd erupted in cheers. "On the morrow, we wed, and she becomes a MacGregor." Men started banging their fists on the table in welcome. "There will be great feasting and celebrations here in the Great Hall afterward, but for now, enjoy a light repast, for I dinnae want you all drunk and stinking of debauchery at me wedding."

The crowd erupted with guffaws, and immediately servers appeared with trenchers of food and ale.

Beiste turned to Amelia and said, "Go with Orla. She will see you to your chambers, where you can rest for the night." Amelia nodded, very much relieved she would get some quiet reprieve from everyone's company. A woman appeared beside her.

Orla

AMELIA HAD TO TAKE a moment to glance at Orla because she had never seen someone who looked like her before. Orla had light brown skin and chestnut-colored hair, but her eyes were a startling greyish green color. She had high cheekbones and tiny freckles and her body; well, it was spectacular. Amelia noted Orla was toned and curvaceous with just the right proportions in contrast to Amelia's short and curvy physique.

Amelia did not realize she was openly staring until Orla said in a defensive tone, "Is there something wrong, Mistress?"

"I am so sorry." Amelia started walking. "Tis just, I have never seen your likeness before. Are all Highland women so well proportioned?"

Orla blushed. "What do you mean?"

"I just want to ken how many women I will have to fight off if they're all as pretty as you."

Orla just grinned.

"Did I say that out loud? Sorry, ignore me, I'm a lowlander. We are, by nature, short, insecure people."

That had Orla chuckling.

Beiste watched his betrothed leave the hall and saw her chatting animatedly with Orla. He also noticed Orla was laughing at something Amelia said. Beiste gave instructions for a platter of food to be taken up to her chambers. In the meantime, he sat down with Dalziel to go over what he had missed while he was away.

Quiet Time

AMELIA GROANED AS SHE sank into the warm bath that had been delivered to her room. She closed her eyes and felt pure bliss after the days of hard riding she had endured. It was such a luxury to have a warm bath. She created a routine of bathing regularly; it was a habit her mother imparted to her; stating it was good to remain clean while treating others with sicknesses. But heated baths were a luxury.

Amelia picked up the soap she had brought with her and scrubbed her entire body from head to toe, rinsing thoroughly. When she was finished, she dried off in front of the roaring fire and donned the clean chemise she found on the bed. It was a bit of a tight squeeze around her breast and bottom, but it was better than wearing a dirty chemise again. Amelia washed her face and scrubbed her teeth with fresh mint and charcoal, rinsing until her mouth felt fresh. She found a long woolen plaid and wrapped it around herself like a shawl, then she brushed her hair by the fireplace. *Pure bliss.* This was a much needed quiet time.

A knock came at the door. When she answered, another woman brought in a large platter of food and drink. Behind her, two retainers appeared to carry out her bath and basins. Then a guard named Donald introduced himself. He informed Amelia that the chieftain's family always had guards watching over them. Amelia was not sure whether that was to stop her from leaving or to keep her safe, but she was too famished to find out. For tonight, she would enjoy her freedom.

Amelia could not believe the decadence. There was fresh fruit, cured meat, bread and cheese. She made her way to the small table and helped herself to the fine fare. The food was tasty, although she noted it could do with certain herbs and salt to make it even more palatable. Either way, the cook was talented. Amelia looked around the room, which was larger than her old cottage, and she was in awe, still coming to terms with what it would mean to be mistress of a large Keep.

Amelia walked over to her chest of things that delivered earlier and took out the oak box. She carefully pulled out the belongings again, stroking the brightly colored *airisaidh* within. She rubbed the crest badge across her fingers and then the brooch. Over the years, she had pulled out the silver brooch when she missed her mother the most. It comforted her.

Amelia wondered if she should wear it tomorrow for her wedding. But her mother said she was to keep it secret until she found her kin. Maybe after the wedding, she would ask her husband if he recognized the plaid and insignia.

Amelia examined the MacGregor plaid that had been left out for her wedding on the morrow and decided she would stick with their traditions for now. There was no point ruffling feathers until she knew more information about who her kin might be.

Amelia carefully placed the items back in the box and locked it. She grabbed a handful of berries wrapped in meat, then wandered about the sizeable chamber, searching for a hiding place while she ate her meal. Amelia eventually found the perfect spot underneath a loose floorboard under the chamber rug. Once the box was secured, she placed the rug back over it. She whispered to the room, "Ma, tis my wedding day tomorrow. I hope your luck shines down on me."

An hour later, Amelia was safely ensconced in the huge, warm bed. She had added more wood to the fire, for it got colder in the Highlands and she snuggled underneath the soft, warm bedding. It was the first time she had felt settled since discovering she was betrothed to the Beast.

Amelia was just drifting off to sleep when the sound of the door opening alerted her. She opened her eyes to see Beiste walking in freshly bathed, hair slightly wet, bare-chested, with nothing but his plaid folded around the belt. He moved straight to the table, poured himself some mead, then moved to the fire, sipping it and warming himself.

Amelia instantly sat up, covering her modesty. "What are you doing here?"

"What does it look like? I've come to sleep," he replied.

"You canna sleep here?"

"Why not? Tis my chambers."

"Your chambers? But, I'm here!"

"So?"

"We are not married yet!"

"Dinnae fash yourself. I will not ravish you, but I will share that bed."

"But this is my time for reflection," she snapped.

Beiste stared at her and chuckled.

"What's so funny, you ogre?" Amelia sat up straighter, glaring daggers at him. Her blanket slipped, revealing a see-through chemise practically wrapped tightly around her ample breasts.

Beiste immediately looked down there and cursed as lust engulfed his senses. He gritted his teeth and replied, "Woman, you can reflect all you like as long as I get to sleep in that bed."

Beiste moved towards her and began unwrapping his plaid.

"What are you doing?" Amelia shrieked.

"I'm undressing to go to sleep, what does it look like?"

"Naked? You are going to sleep naked?" There went her high-pitched voice again.

"Aye, I'll not wear dirty travel clothes to bed," Beiste growled.

By this time, Amelia's panic was genuine. "Do you mean to tell me that in all the rooms in this huge Keep you could not find any clean clothes to sleep in?" she asked half shouting.

"No, I could not. Now sheath your claws she-cat, I'm getting a headache."

Before Amelia could protest any further, Beiste dropped his plaid onto the floor, threw the bedcovers back, and climbed into bed.

Amelia covered her eyes. "I cannot believe you. This is sacrilegious."

"Quiet. Some of us are trying to sleep," Beiste grumbled and turned his back to her, fluffing up his pillow exaggeratedly. He could hear Amelia huffing and Beiste just bit back a laugh. *Lord, how he loved to raise her ire.* Beiste relaxed and feigned sleep while Amelia kept fuming.

Her peaceful night of reflection shattered. Amelia glared at Beiste's back imagining all kinds of ways to murder him, stabbing him in the arm, smothering him with her pillow, burning him with the fire poker. Then an idea came to her. *Find another room.* Yes, that is what she would do. She would retrieve her plaid and go out and ask Donald to direct her to another room. Donald was her guard, and it was his duty to see to things like this.

Her mind made up, Amelia flung her legs over the side of the bed and was about to stand then yelped when an enormous arm grabbed her around her middle and hauled her back into bed. Within seconds a very naked Beiste had her tucked into his very naked side, one arm draped over her body to keep her in place and his thigh entwined with hers. He pulled the covers back over them and muttered, "Stop thinking overly much and go to sleep, wench."

"I dinnae want to sleep with you." Amelia scowled.

"Methinks, you protest too much."

"I dinnae protest!"

"Good, then tis settled, go to sleep," Beiste growled.

"Humf."

Beiste quietly chuckled. It felt good having Amelia in his arms again. He had every intention of sleeping elsewhere but he had gotten used to sharing a pallet with her so against his better judgment he decided to just continue as he meant to go on. Beiste tucked Amelia closer to his side and settled again. He breathed in her lilac scent and drifted off to sleep.

Amelia was part outraged but mostly exhausted. Besides, it felt nice and warm, tucked up against Beiste, even if he was naked. Before long, she too welcomed slumber's warm embrace.

⁂

THE CLOAKED FIGURE continued to move in the shadows, contemplating his next move. He was struck by how comely the new wife was and even more so at how she handled the Beast. He would have to tread carefully. Caitrin was weak and easily frightened, this one had a backbone. Still, he would enjoy breaking her. He licked his lips and adjusted his trews. No doubt he would be sure to sample her before she died.

Chapter 11

The Wedding

Amelia awoke to an empty bed on her wedding day. It relieved her to have the morning to herself. She slept so well during the night she was feeling well-rested. She carried out her morning routine, washing her face, using the privy, which it pleased her was clean and only for their use. Amelia partook of a light breakfast and not long afterward, a procession of women entered her chambers to prepare her for her wedding. She was bathed and scrubbed within an inch of her life, her hair was brushed and styled.

Amelia had expected to see Orla, but it was Deidre, Jonet's maid, who attended to dress her. Deidre wore a severe face, and every time she smiled, it did not quite reach her eyes. She helped Amelia get dressed in a long silk kirtle and the MacGregor *airisaidh*.

Now and then, Deidre would make cutting remarks about Amelia's size and how they should probably readjust the seams, for she was bigger than Beiste's usual taste in women, but Amelia refused to let it bother her.

Later, a guardsman named Alasdair introduced himself. He had relieved Donald and would be with her for the day.

Soon, word came that the priest was ready. Amelia stepped outside of her chambers and took a deep breath. Servants were standing on the landing, smiling at her and wishing her well as she descended the stairs. Her step faltered for a second. She thought she saw the figure in a grey cloak standing among them. Goosebumps formed along her arm, but when she looked again; he was gone. She figured she must be seeing things. It must be her nerves. She resumed walking as Alasdair led her down the stairs to the Great Hall.

THE CLOAKED ONE WATCHED *from a distance. In all the festivities, he was invisible, hidden in plain sight, easily able to blend in and move with freedom. He had been watching her with interest and curiosity from the shadows. She was comely and buxom and made to please a man like him. He had planned to watch her sleep, but the Beast had joined her himself and placed a guard at the door. No doubt the Beast had rutted her luscious body like a whore the whole night. He was angry the Beast received the best of everything. But patience is a virtue. He would bide his time. His turn would come, and then he would strike.*

Dark Thoughts

BEISTE LEFT AMELIA'S chamber after a very restful sleep. He was not sure when it happened, but he had no night terrors since leaving *Dunbar*. When Amelia was in his arms, he slept well. As he descended the stairs to ready himself for the wedding, he realized he was getting married again and he did not mind so much.

He tried to remember what it was like with his first wedding. Caitrin was the daughter of a neighboring clan laird, and they had barely spoken even during the courting stage. She was quiet, never raised her voice, and always agreed with him. But no matter what he did, she was always terrified of everything, even her own shadow. Their wedding night had been awkward and the few times they coupled was purely to create an heir, which was all she wanted, a bairn. When she was with child, Beiste was so relieved that he would not have to bed her again, and now he felt guilty about that.

Was it right that he was now about to start a life with someone else? The guilt crept in. Since meeting Amelia, he had not thought about Caitrin. He had not thought about the bairn he had lost and the wife who killed herself. Beiste was forgetting what she even looked like and sounded like. He should have been here with her that night. He should never have left her, so he could fight some ridiculous skirmish. Darkness plagued Beiste's mood as he made his way to the chapel.

Here Comes the Bride

THE BARD PLAYED A SLOW tune as Amelia walked into the chapel. They gave Brodie the honors of walking her down the aisle. When he greeted her, he just beamed and said, "You look bonnie, Mistress."

Amelia walked down the aisle with Brodie but with no family on her side; she felt sad about that. *What of her mother's kin? Would they have wanted to be present if they knew her?* She looked around the chapel. Someone had tastefully decorated it with flowers; they had clean rushes on the floor. So many thoughts went through Amelia's mind. She could only hope her new clan accepted her.

Amelia stared ahead and smiled at Beiste. A shadow crossed over his face, and he frowned.

She paused, but Brodie kept walking. "It will be all right, Mistress, just wedding nerves."

By the time she reached Beiste, he wore a stony expression. Brodie held out her hand for Beiste to take, but Beiste hesitated.

"Mistress, if things dinnae work out with Beiste, I am always free," Brodie whispered.

Beiste pulled Amelia away from Brodie's arm and said, "Go away."

Brodie released her and replied, "I was just letting her ken, she always has choices."

Amelia glanced up at Beiste and he was facing the priest, looking tense, but he had her hand firmly gripped in his.

"Are you all right, Beiste? Is something wrong?" she whispered.

"Let's get this over with, shall we?" he replied.

They took their vows. Beiste was tense throughout the wedding. Amelia knew if she let his behavior affect her, she was likely to weep and embarrass herself in front of his clan. Instead, she kept a stony silence throughout and refused to look at him. When it was time to kiss, she pecked his cheek and turned away. The priest announced them, husband and wife. The crowd roared and celebrations began.

Amelia just felt empty inside.

Back in the Great Hall, Beiste tried to shake the maudlin thoughts about Caitrin, but they kept intruding. He drank more ale and tried to relax, then he looked over at his wife. *His wife.* He still could not believe Amelia was his. Then he noticed she seemed detached and quiet. The sparkle in her eyes had dimmed, and he kicked himself for his own selfishness. It was not her fault they forced her to wed.

He remembered the moment she walked down the aisle, all else faded. Her loveliness stirred something deep within his soul and no matter how much he tried, it just burrowed deeper. Then the guilt encroached on his feelings, and he had blamed her.

Beiste grabbed Amelia's chair and pulled it with her closer towards him. She startled and peered up at him. Before she could say a word, he leaned closer and kissed her deep and long. He stroked her mouth with his tongue, mimicking the act they would soon partake of with other parts of their bodies.

Amelia stiffened at first, but then relaxed into him. She could not resist. Her skin was on fire, a feeling she had never experienced before, and she opened to him.

She moved closer, needed more from Beiste, but knew not what. He deepened his kiss. Then picked her up and sat her on his lap, their mouths still fused together.

People began cheering, and they separated and laughed, but not before Beiste looked at her and said, "You are a beautiful, Amelia. I should have mentioned that earlier. Forgive my failure to do so."

His eyes held genuine remorse, and Amelia nodded. They turned back to the crowd who had called out for a toast, then the festivities began.

THAT NIGHT THEY STOOD in their bedchamber and Beiste could not wait another second to make Amelia his wife in all ways.

"I need to ken if you have coupled with any other before me," he asked.

Amelia shook her head.

"Then we will go slow, my love," he said. Even though he knew it would kill him.

Beiste removed her chemise slowly whilst ravishing her mouth. He bared her luscious breasts to his gaze and growled. Wherever his eyes roamed, his hands, lips and tongue followed. Amelia threw her head back and moaned.

Beiste promised he would go slow, but the sounds she was making were feeding a primal need to claim and conquer. Amelia shrieked in surprise when Beiste picked her up and unceremoniously threw her on the bed, spreading her legs wide for his view.

Amelia tried to cover herself, but he would not let her. "No, you are mine. Dinnae ever hide yourself from me!"

Beiste removed his clothes and joined her. He explored her entire body with his lips and tongue, all the while his thumb rubbed the center of her heat. Her breaths became sharp gasps as Beiste lowered his head to her breast and suckled a hardened peak. The sensations were overwhelming.

Amelia felt the pressure building from her nipple to her molten core. Like a crescendo seeking its ultimate peak, her body stiffened, then she shouted her release. Beiste did not stop his relentless assault. He hovered above her creating friction and pressure at her center, where his hard length now replaced his thumb. Amelia spread her thighs wider, needing more, pleading with her eyes for something only he could give. She gripped his forearms.

Beiste complied, and in one hard thrust he broke through her barrier and sheathed himself within her welcoming heat. He stilled. His brow furrowed with concern as his lips hovered an inch away from hers. "Are you all right, Love?"

She nodded her head. "I need you to move now."

Beiste claimed her with a visceral need, he increased his pace as her breasts bounced with the power of each thrust.

Amelia could feel every inch of her husband inside her. The euphoric rise began again as they became one, skin against skin, flesh against flesh. Beiste took her with wild abandon, no more control or finesse. They climaxed together as he roared his release and bathed her womb with his seed.

Beiste lay in thrall to a peaceful, contented feeling. Amelia was passed out with pleasure beside him. He knew then he was in danger of becoming enamored with his wife. He needed to create space between them, tomorrow he would start. Tonight he would savor the comfort a little longer.

THE CLOAKED ONE HOVERED in the shadows of the hallway, far enough away so the guards could not see but close enough he could hear the noises coming from the chamber. So, the Beast and his bride were one. He heard enough of the moaning and grunting coming from their room to know they engaged in the marriage's consummation.

He shook his head. At the rate they were going, it would not take long for their union to create an heir. That was something he would never allow. He moved back towards the wall leading to the secret passageway.

It was time to give his minion below stairs a visit; she was failing in her duty. He would need to punish her the only way she understood. It would be painful for her, but pleasurable for him especially since the noises from the chamber had made him feral.

Chapter 12

The Morning After

Amelia woke from blissful slumber cocooned in warmth. She tried to get up before realizing a firm body lay curled behind her. One arm lay across her waist and one leg was draped over her thigh. *Beiste's.* They were on their side, her head tucked up under his chin, and he slept soundly. She tried to move away, but his arm tightened.

"No," he growled. Then he fell back to sleep. Amelia tried to shift her leg out from under him, but again, he tightened his embrace and growled. Even while asleep, the man was annoying, she thought. With a resigned sigh, Amelia decided to just wait until he awoke. She felt sore in parts she never thought could feel sore.

Her mind drifted to the day before and the wedding night. *Lud, what a night.* It was positively wicked and exhausting. But she would have no problem doing it all again. She yawned at that thought and drifted into oblivion.

Beiste woke with a start and feeling the most refreshed he had ever felt in a long time. He had an instant awareness of the woman in his arms and the fragrance of her hair. *His wife.* His hot, passionate, responsive wife. He took a deep breath of satisfaction, feeling Amelia in his arms, and tightened his hold around her. He thought of all the wonderful things he would love to do with her. She was a quick study in bed play, but not today. She would be sore, and she needed soothing. He caught himself smiling.

Beiste grimaced at the realization that this woman utterly beguiled him. He thought she was an obsession he could work out of his system, but Amelia was slowly digging her way under his skin. He knew this much dependency on a female could ruin him. It was a path he had never trodden before and the best way to ensure he kept some clarity was to keep some emotional distance between them.

The first step was to not laze about in bed, enjoying her kisses and company. He needed to leave now before she woke up; he rolled out of bed and grabbed his plaid. But he was too late because he heard a sleepy voice greet him, "Good morning, Husband."

Beiste turned to see Amelia sitting up in bed blushing, trying to hold the surrounding bedcovers. She looked so delectable and well and truly tumbled. So sweet and so innocent after a night of unadulterated ravishment. He frowned again. He needed to get out of there.

"Wife, there is much to do today. We need to fly the bloodied sheet as proof we have consummated the marriage," he said gruffly. Beiste registered the flicker of hurt in her eyes once she realized what he meant, and he regretted his words. But Amelia had already shuttered her features.

He moved to soothe her but stopped himself. "Are you well?" he asked.

She nodded her head.

"Then dinnae lie abed long. There is much to do." Without another word, Beiste donned his plaid and walked out of the room. Shouting orders as he descended the stairs.

All the gentleness was gone with the morning light. Amelia fumed at her husband's mood swing. As if she was the one lying abed without his behemoth body trapping her. She would have been out and about a long time ago; she was not lazy, and she was not idle. With her resolve firmly in place, Amelia jumped out of bed and decided to ignore her husband from now on.

Just then, a knock came at the door. It was a maid. "Excuse me, Mistress, the chieftain has sent up a hot bath for you and we will need the sheets for the tower."

Amelia blushed at the thought of the whole Keep having to see her virginal blood flapping in the breeze as a sign that the marriage was now fully enforceable. She realised then that Beiste just needed her compliant to prove his claim on her dowry and that parcel of land.

Amelia felt an ache in her heart as reality set in. This was the fate of women, merely a means to an end. Her entire life, she had been nothing more than a means to an end. *Why did she expect anything would be different now?*

Two women came in and hung the sheet for the world to see.

Lady's Maid

AMELIA WAS SURPRISED to see Orla again. She stood with toweling and fresh water, bussed around the chamber, setting things right and stoking the fire. Amelia also noticed the strange accent she spoke. It was like the *Norn* of old. She would have to ask her someday about her heritage. Amelia was not used to having servants, but she thanked Orla as she enjoyed the warm bath. As they chatted, Amelia decided she liked Orla.

After Amelia had finished her bath and was dressed, Orla was helping her manage her unruly hair when she asked, "Mistress, would you like me to attend to you each morning or help you in any way? Twould be my honor to serve you?"

"Thank you, Orla, but I think I can manage on my own. I am not used to having help."

Orla's face dropped. "I understand." She put on a forced smile and hovered by the door as men arrived to remove the bath.

When the door opened again, Deidre walked in and held a haughty expression. "Mistress." She curtsied at Amelia. "Lady Jonet sent me to assist you." Deidre turned to see Orla, and Amelia caught her sneer.

"I apologize, Mistress, but there seems to have been a mistake. I am your assistant today, not Orla." Deidre then commanded, "Orla, come with me."

Both women stepped outside and closed the door.

Amelia found the exchange peculiar and having such an inquisitive nature, she quietly ran to the door to listen in and sure enough, she could hear their conversation outside. She spied down the keyhole to see better. *Eavesdropping,* that is what they called it in Dunbar. She learned that from a crofter. He used to say, "No secrets can be discovered by just lying around waiting for it to hit your ears." She had to agree. Amelia leaned closer to hear better.

"Orla, how dare you attend the mistress?" Deidre snapped.

"I was only doing what the chieftain asked me yestereve," Orla replied.

"He must be mistaken. He has been very distracted lately or he would never have put the bastard of a Viking's whore in here," Deidre hissed.

Orla bristled. "You ken nothing about my parents."

"Neither do you... *orphan.*"

Something about the conversation raised Amelia's hackles. She knew what it was like to have people call your mother a whore.

Orla replied, "Tis better than being a hacket bitch!"

Deidre slapped Orla hard across the face. Amelia could just make out Orla's eyes water.

It was then she made up her mind. Amelia opened the door abruptly. "Orla, what on earth is taking you so long? I have been waiting for an age for you to assist me."

Orla looked confused. "Sorry, Mistress... I am not sure —"

Amelia saw the sting on Orla's cheek and said, "Well, come on then, are you going to do my hair or not? I told you I need someone to help me in the mornings. Have you forgotten?" She made an impatient gesture for Orla to step inside. Once Orla crossed the threshold, Amelia turned to Deidre and said, "Thank you, but I have chosen Orla to assist me." With that, Amelia shut the door in Deidre's face.

"Thank you, Mistress, but I dinnae think I should help. Tis not my place," Orla said.

"Nonsense. Was it not the chieftain who sent you?"

"Well, yes, but —"

"Then he must have had a good reason. I will not overturn his decision."

"Are you in earnest?"

"Aye, truth is, I need help. I have never been in this position before."

"Then it will be my pleasure to serve you." Orla took a deep breath and straightened her shoulders and smiled.

"What do you ken of Deidre?" Amelia asked.

"She was lady's maid to the late mistress, Caitrin, and after she died, Deidre moved in to help lady Jonet."

"What is Deidre like?"

"She seems to keep to herself, but she just does not like me." Orla shrugged.

Amelia pondered it while she sat quietly as Orla expertly donned her hair and dressed her in a blue *airisaidh* with a white linen long-sleeved shirt inside and a warm hose underneath.

"Orla, this looks lovely. I hardly recognized myself."

"You look, exquisite, Mistress."

"Please call me Amelia."

"I cannot. It would be disrespectful."

"What if you called me Amelia when tis just us?"

"Aye, I can do that," Orla replied.

"Orla, if you dinnae mind me asking, where does your clan hale from? Your features I have never seen the likeness before."

"Tis all right Mistr... I mean Amelia. I am an outsider, really. I was an orphan and after five summers, they left me to be raised by Morag."

"Morag, the healer?"

"Aye. She believes my da to be a Norseman, though she could never confirm it. My ma was most likely a slave from a far-off land... I ken not."

"Twould explain your slight accent. tis subtle but still there. Do you remember any of your kin when you were a bairn?"

"Most of it was a blur. But I remember sitting atop the shoulders of an enormous man with long golden hair and he spoke in a tongue I used to ken but cannot remember now. I still hope that someday he will return for me, but I ken this cannot be. He didna want me to begin with. Why would he want me now?"

Amelia noticed Orla staring into the distance out the window, a look of longing upon her face. Amelia understood the feeling well. Although she was fortunate, she had her mother and knew who her father was, but that yearning to find a place to belong was a difficult void to fill. She spoke before she thought better of it.

"I lost my ma when I was fifteen summers old. Before she died, she told me I had kin here in the Highlands. I hope someday I will find them. Tis as if something has been missing, not kenning who they are."

Orla nodded in understanding.

"Orla, would you like to be my lady's maid?"

"I would love it above anything else," Orla replied.

"Then tis done. Where do you stay? In the Keep?"

"No, I live in the cottage in the woods with Morag. I help her when I can."

"Morag lives in the woods?"

"Aye, she prefers to commune with nature."

"I think tis time I went to meet Morag for I have missed the woods a great deal. Will you take me to her after we break our fast?"

"Of course."

At breakfast in the Great Hall, Amelia sat with her mother-in-law Jonet and a very silent Sorcha. Both women smiled, then continued eating quietly. Amelia could not help but grimace at Jonet's gruel. It looked terrible and had an unpleasant odor. She made a mental note to find out if there was any way she could improve Jonet's diet, for it did not look like it tasted any better.

Amelia noticed Beiste had not appeared, but then a lot of his men were also missing. She was to find out later that the men had already broken their fast as they had an early ride out to a neighboring clan for trade.

It embarrassed Amelia that she had to learn of her husband's movements from everyone else except the brute in question. Donning a decent dress for the first time in her life, she fashioned a headscarf and was out the door with Orla, sleeves rolled up, ready to start her day.

Amelia Meets the Oracle

AMELIA FOLLOWED ORLA to Morag's cottage. Orla chatted the whole way, pointed out things around the Keep as they entered the woods.

Amelia noticed there was a guard not far off who had followed her. His name was Alasdair. She had met him before and knew he was on duty to make sure she did not get into any mischief or run away. *Huh, as if she had any inclination to do that.*

As they made to enter the woods, Alasdair cautioned, "Mistress, I would advise against going too far from the Keep. Where is it you wish to venture?"

"She is going with me to see Morag..."

"You go to see the Oracle?"

"Aye."

Alasdair stared for a while at both women and nodded his head, but this time he walked in front of them with a hand to his sword, scouting out the territory as they trailed behind.

Amelia was even more intrigued, but she followed while she and Orla chatted quietly. It amazed her how much knowledge Orla possessed about almost every detail within Keep and village life. Amelia was even more certain that she had chosen well, making Orla her lady's maid. The woman was knowledgeable, informative, but also knew when to be quiet and just observe. It was usually the people who lived on the edges of society who could glean the most information, and Orla showed no reluctance to share as much with Amelia as she could.

It took only a brief walk over a crest, and they could see a small, quaint cottage with smoke rising from the chimney. Amelia saw it and felt homesick, for it reminded her of her cottage in *Dunbar*. She felt a chilled wind rake the back of her neck, which had her shivering for a moment, then she shook it off and continued to walk. To her surprise, the door opened, and Amelia could see inside an elderly woman sitting at a table. Alasdair stepped through first, looked around, greeted the old woman, then ventured outside and ushered Amelia and Orla in whilst still looking around the woods.

Amelia smiled and greeted the old woman, expecting someone to be behind the door, but there was no one. She shivered slightly again, but deferred to Orla to make the introductions.

Before anything else could be said, the old woman stood up and, with a smooth voice that belied her years, said, "Hello child, you are late."

"I'm sorry?"

"I expected you a lot sooner," Morag muttered.

"Well, I only just learned you were Orla's ma this morning, and I—"

"Och, but I have kenned about you for a vera long time."

"I suppose so. I would like to thank you for the rose-honey."

"No need to thank me, Mistress. I kenned you would need it."

"But how did you ken it would be me and not my sister, who would marry the chieftain?"

"Sometimes I just see what is revealed for me to see."

Orla walked towards Morag and kissed her cheek. She bade Amelia sit down while she got busy brewing tea. "Come now, Ma, stop speaking in riddles or you'll chase my new mistress away."

The old woman clucked her teeth at her adopted daughter, but Amelia could see it was done affectionately. There was a lot of love between them. "Vera well. I am glad you have made my lass your maid. She will become a greater friend to you than you can ever imagine right now."

"But how did you ken? I only met Orla this morn."

"Och child, pay attention and you too will ken things before others do."

"Ma, you are doing it again," Orla said and rolled her eyes.

"Och, go on with you and stop harassing an old lady."

Amelia sat and chatted more. She already felt at home in this little cottage and, with the warm brew warming her belly, she relaxed.

They talked of many things when Morag suddenly gripped Amelia's arm and said in an otherworldly voice, "Your kin will come for you. Keep watch, for evil has already arrived." She let go of Amelia's arm and continued chatting as if nothing had happened.

Amelia stilled, not quite knowing what to make of it. *Why would the Dunbars come for her?* She leaned back and resumed her calm composure, but she was beginning to wonder if Morag really was a witch.

Chapter 13

Rules of Engagement

For several days, Beiste continued to treat Amelia with a distance and a coldness during the day that she could not understand. However, they still shared the same bedchamber at night. She tried to sleep in her own room to give him his own space, but Beiste just carried her back to their bed. That was the strange thing. For all the coldness he displayed towards her during the day, their nights were the complete opposite and filled with fire and passion. Amelia knew at some point they would need to talk about it, until then she would go on, undeterred.

It was a beautiful day and Amelia and Orla headed out to an abandoned cottage not too far from the Keep but also close enough to the woods where she could forage. Dalziel had mentioned to her the cottage was available if she wanted to move some of her herbs and seedlings there, and she had been grateful for his thoughtfulness. That was one thing she was learning about Dalziel. He was extremely quiet, but he was observant and considerate. Beiste had also taken to sending two men with her everywhere she went so they could guard and assist if she needed any help. She had Donald and Fergus guarding her this day.

Amelia was busy planting her herbs while Orla remained close, sharing all the Keep gossip and fashioning a bow out of sinews for her steelhead arrows. Amelia had discovered that Orla was quite a skilled bowyer. She had apprenticed with the local weapons master at Morag's insistence. The weapons master had at first balked at the idea of training a girl, but after threats of a hex and other curses from Morag, he relented. Orla was now fashioning a bow for Amelia.

Amelia, with Donald's help, had already cordoned off sections of the garden for distinct types of plants. Fergus would have none of it. He kept watch and did not budge from his post.

While Amelia was digging, she saw Sorcha standing nearby, watching.

"Come, you are always welcome here, Sister. Dinnae be afraid."

Sorcha nodded, then slowly made her way toward her. Amelia noticed Sorcha was still uncomfortable around her, but rather than push, she kept talking and continued planting seedlings, taking them out of the small containers she had fashioned out of the bracken.

"Now this plant here is Herb Robert. It helps control bleeding. Over there are stinging nettles. When they are dried and mixed with other plants, they make a soothing tea that can help ease pain. And here is yarrow. It helps stop bleeding on the inside."

Sorcha looked as if an unknown world opened for her as she gazed at the array of plants and seedlings.

"Would you like to help me?" Amelia asked.

Sorcha's face immediately lit up, and she nodded profusely with an even bigger smile, eager to learn. Soon Sorcha was planting and digging alongside Amelia.

"Sorcha, has anyone tried to communicate with you beyond hand gestures?" Amelia asked. Sorcha shook her head.

"Would you like me to teach you a way?" Amelia whispered to her. Sorcha nodded. "All right, but it must be our secret."

That afternoon, in the guise of gardening, Amelia taught Sorcha how to read and write. Starting with letters in the dirt. Amelia had yet to tell Beiste of her skill, but in time, she would.

BEISTE AND BRODIE SAT atop the hill on horseback, staring down at the cottage. Beiste did this several times a day, just seeking Amelia out, making sure she was all right and safe. Seeing her with his sister made his heart feel light because she took the time with Sorcha when others had no patience. His decision to wed her seemed an even better one.

Brodie broke his reverie. "She is good with her," he said.

"Aye, she is."

"You are a lucky man to find a kind wife. She has a gentleness about her that Sorcha responds to. Even Jonet seeks her out whenever she is around."

"She has been a boon for both of them," Beiste replied.

"I dare say she has been a boon for you too."

Beiste said nothing. He did not want to admit out loud how glad he was that he had married Amelia instead of Mary.

"So why dinnae you just go say hello instead of stalking her from afar?" Brodie asked.

"I dinnae stalk my wife."

Brodie chuckled, "Whatever you say..."

"I dinnae stalk her!"

"Then why do you insist we ride up here every day at the same time and do nothing else but stare at that patch of dirt she calls a garden?"

Beiste scowled. "Shut up, you ass. I didna ask you to come with me."

"Aye, you did." Brodie mimicked Beiste's deep, gruff voice. "Brodie, we need to ride to the ridge so I can stalk my bonnie wife, imagining all the different ways I can lick her sweet —"

Brodie didn't get a chance to finish that sentence because, without warning, Beiste knocked him off his horse. Brodie hit the grass with a loud thud and howled with laughter.

Beiste rode past him and muttered, "Dumb prick."

Brodie chuckled, picked himself up, dusted himself off, then walked towards his horse. When he had mounted, his eyes were drawn back to the scene below, in particular to Orla.

Orla the Orphan, the bane of Brodie's existence. *She was a beauty,* he thought. It was such a pity she detested him so much. He wondered what it would be like for Orla to look at him with something other than derision. Brodie shook his head. *Why the devil did he care*? She was a nobody, a no one, nothing. He told that lie to himself daily.

Ranalf

IT WAS AT THE EVENING meal that night in the Great Hall when Amelia noticed something interesting about Ranalf, one of her new guardsmen. He kept staring at Orla like he was ravenous, and she was a succulent piece of venison. The intensity was there. Amelia also noticed Deidre trying hard to garner Ranalf's attention. She wore a low-cut gown, making sure her bosoms would brush across his arm as she served wine to the guards and retainers. Ranalf seemed oblivious. Never taking his gaze off Orla.

So, that was why Deidre was hostile towards Orla. Deidre wanted Ranalf, and he wanted Orla.

Amelia wondered whether Orla had feelings for Ranalf? She was still staring when Beiste turned her head and planted a searing kiss on her lips, then said, "Cease looking at Ranalf or so help me, I will run him through. You are mine!" His eyes were blazing.

"I was not staring," Amelia replied in outrage. Beiste turned away and ignored her, speaking to Dalziel instead.

Amelia was getting a sore neck from his constant mood swings.

Beiste sat quietly, listening to Dalziel, yet he was aware of everything regarding his wife. He was not jealous, he never got jealous over a woman, but if she looked at Ranalf one more time, he would throw her over his shoulder and march her back up to their chambers.

Amelia continued to watch Orla and saw Ranalf finally make his move to sit next to her. Orla smiled up at him and they began conversing. Amelia heard a cup slam down hard onto the table from the opposite side. It was Brodie, glaring at Orla. He did not look happy at all. *What was that about?*

Amelia watched as Brodie stood and moved towards Orla and Ranalf. Brodie said something to Ranalf and Ranalf did not look happy. He turned to Orla, excused himself, and then walked out of the hall. Brodie then walked back to the dais, not saying a word.

Orla stared at Brodie in shock, then she gave Amelia a confused look.

What was wrong with the absurd men in this Keep?

Alone Again

IT WAS DIFFICULT FOR the residents of the Keep to comprehend what had changed between the chieftain and his new wife. In the first month of their marriage, people noticed a distance growing between them. It saddened Amelia that once again; she felt destined to belong nowhere. Beiste seemed to behave even more detached. If they passed each other in the hallway, he would barely even acknowledge her. His ardor for her at night remained strong. In fact, they had not spent a single night apart, but even that was wearing thin.

Maybe men were different. They could separate the physical from the emotional. Amelia was discovering she could not. She had become less responsive to his touch, and she feared in time they would not even share their nights. Beiste, she had to admit, could hurt her deeply, and she knew not how to protect herself from the pain.

And so it was. One morning after Beiste had left their bed having spoken nary a word, Orla tried to explain to Amelia some of what she knew of the Beast.

"Dinnae worry overmuch, Amelia. From what I see, he is very much enamored with you. Tis just the way of men. They are fools of the first order."

"It still hurts, though, Orla. I just wish I had kenned how to break through whatever this need is he has for distance. I dinnae mean to be a needy wife, but we could achieve so much more if we worked together."

"I ken tis not my place, but tis rumored Beiste still mourns his first wife. Mayhap tis what plays on his mind? Most people ken he became a lot harsher after Caitrin passed. Tis why he never let the thing with Elora go any further."

"Elora?" Amelia asked.

"Oh, forgive me. I did not mean to bring that up, it just slipped… it went nowhere." Orla looked worried.

"Please tell me, Orla, what of him and Elora? I ken she always gives me dagger eyes whenever she sees me."

"I tell you this, so you ken not to trust some women here. A year after the old mistress passed, Beiste kept to himself. He never dallied, though many a female tried to tempt him. Tis rumored he must have missed his wife something fierce. Then one night, he caved and took Elora as his lover. She waited for him in his bed, naked, hoping to entice him out of his celibacy."

Amelia did not like the thought of that. She wanted to scratch the woman's eyes out.

Orla continued. "But the affair was short-lived, and Beiste never returned to her bed or anyone else's again. Elora believes she still has a hold over him, but from what I've seen, there is no way, definitely not since he married you."

Amelia felt bereft, and she did not know why. She, a daughter of a leman, should have prepared for something like this, but it still stung being a wife and having no real claim to her husband. She had to compete with a dead woman he still loved and a past lover who hovered about the place like a foul smell. Amelia knew things had to change between them and she would confront this matter head-on.

That night, when Beiste quietly came to her, Amelia made sure she was sitting by the fire. She wanted to talk to him and lay some ground rules of what she needed. Not this coldness between them.

Suffice to say, it did not go well.

When Beiste reached for her, Amelia stopped him and said, "Husband, we need to talk, please."

"I would prefer we did things other than talk," Beiste grumbled.

"I dinnae ken why the cool indifference towards me?"

When Beiste realized he would not get his way so easily, he lashed out. "Because, wife, if I had a choice, I would not marry so soon after losing Caitrin."

Amelia flinched at the accusatory tone, but Beiste continued. "My hand was forced, and I admit, so was yours." Beiste tried to remain calm. He could not think properly. He had had a bad day and just wanted to lose himself inside his wife. It was the only peace he found. "I think if you tamed your tongue and curbed your temper, we could get on well with mutual respect for the purpose of producing my heirs," he snapped.

"What am I to expect from you in return when you want nothing to do with me during the day?" Amelia asked.

"I will protect and provide for you as my wife, and I expect us to couple often. Beyond the bedchamber, we would not have to spend too much time together. You will respect me in public and in front of my men, and I will do the same."

"Those are your rules?" Amelia asked.

"Aye, they are. Abide by those boundaries and we will get on well. Otherwise, I answer to no one. I do as I please."

"And what am I to do all day while I wait around for you to bed me?"

"Whatever it is you have been doing so far. I expect you to take over the running of the Keep and household. Deidre is chatelain in Ma's stead, but it is high time you took over. Everything else is in my domain. I make the ultimate decisions here."

Amelia stood up and began pacing. "So, my duty is to run the household and produce heirs, and beyond those two areas, I am to ask for nothing else?"

Beiste folded his arms, stood his ground and said, "Aye. That should not be hard to do."

Amelia decided if they were talking about boundaries, then she would lay some of her own. She stopped pacing and asked him, "Do you have any by-blows?"

He was startled but shook his head. "No, if I did, I would acknowledge them. I have been careful in my relations with women not to leave them with bairns."

"And do you still have relations with other women?" Amelia asked, raising an eyebrow.

"Not since I wed you, Wife, as you ken. I have been in our bed every night."

"What of the day, Husband? When I am not around? Will you still have relations with other women when the need arises?"

Beiste said nothing. He just clenched his jaw and stared at her with an expressionless mask of indifference.

Amelia could feel her temper rising at his silence. She gritted her teeth and asked, "Then let me put it another way, Husband. Do you expect me to be faithful to my vows?"

He growled, "I want my heirs to be of my loins and I will kill any man you take up with."

"Then will you be faithful to your vows?" she asked.

"That is none of your concern."

"So, you intend to break your vows but expect me to keep mine? You intend to sully our marriage bed?"

Beiste did not understand where this conversation was going. The woman was making him daft. But now he was angry that she questioned him at all. "Men do as they please. Wives obey!"

Amelia saw red. "I see. Then you can take your vows and stick it to the devil!" she shouted at him.

"Dinnae tell me what to do with my life, Amie," he replied.

"I am a healer and sicknesses are carried when men dally. If you cannot keep me safe in that regard, then I care not who you sleep with because it will not be me!" Amelia yelled and with that declaration, she ran to her own chambers, slammed the door, locked it, and pushed her trunk across it.

"Wife, come back here!" Beiste roared. He was banging on the door, and she could hear him trying to push it open, but then he just gave up. "Fine, you want to be that way. Dinnae blame me if I seek my pleasure elsewhere!"

Amelia wanted to cry. He had just described a broodmare. There would be no affection or feeling. She would even have to share her husband and just be alone all over again.

For the next three days, Amelia made herself scarce. She avoided Beiste and made sure she was always busy. Amelia had taken to sleeping in her chamber and locking the door. She was done. Amelia realized she needed to adjust to her circumstances; she had been lulled into a false sense of safety with this marriage, but she should have learned she had no one to rely on but herself. Having a husband changed nothing.

Beiste was furious that Amelia would have nothing to do with him. She would not even speak to him, and he could never bloody find her. Wanting to make sure she understood she had no hold on him. He was not sure why he did it, but he invited Elora to sit at the dais and eat with the family that night. No woman would hold him hostage with their demands. He wanted to show Amelia how easily she could be replaced, and he would do as he pleased.

Beiste heard the murmurings of dissension when he did it. Elora beamed with pride sitting next to him and looking down her nose at everyone. And he knew then he had made a monumental mistake.

Amelia finally came down to the Great Hall, and she stilled. She stared at Elora, who gave her a catty smile, and at her husband. Pure anguish marred her countenance, but she would not back away. Amelia straightened her spine, walked over to Jonet, who looked confused, and sat down between her and Sorcha. The latter was staring daggers at her brother.

Both Dalziel and Brodie did not look happy, either. Orla looked like she wanted to claw Elora's eyes out. But no one said anything.

Elora was oblivious to the tension and kept touching Beiste's arm.

Beiste realized then he had shamed his wife publicly, the last thing he ever wanted to do, and he was tired of Elora touching him. It felt like a thousand viper bites across his skin. It was so unwelcome. What he wanted to do was apologize to Amelia, but she would not look at him. She just stared down at her food and said not a word.

THAT NIGHT, WHILE BEISTE stayed in the hall with his doxy, as Amelia now referred to her, she made plans with Orla.

Orla excused herself early and left the hall. When Amelia returned to her own chambers, Orla was already inside, waiting for her. Orla had retrieved Amelia's box from Beiste's room as per her instructions.

Amelia decided it was time she found out more information about her kin. Now that she was in the Highlands, it would make finding them easier. Amelia planned to leave this place and that ox of a husband. She would not live like her mother had, always waiting for the meagre crumbs a man would offer. Amelia would not live that way. She needed to see Morag, but she did not want any guards with her.

Twenty minutes later, Orla emerged from Amelia's chambers dressed like her, with extra padding in her clothes and with a hood over her head. She walked out of the Keep. The guards followed Orla. Amelia then slipped out, dressed in a plain tunic and airisaidh to cover her face.

Amelia made her way to the woods with the box tucked under her arm. She wanted far away from the Keep and Beiste and whatever harem he set up.

When she arrived at Morag's cottage, the door opened before she could knock. "Och child, I kenned you would come here soon. The Beast is a fool. He fights against what he canna control. He will learn soon enough the way to win is to lose."

Amelia just smiled. Of course, Morag already knew she was coming. "Morag, I need help with something and I dinnae ken, who else to ask."

"Tis about your kin?"

"Aye. I need to find my ma's kin. It was a promise I made but never fulfilled and well now I feel the need to ken their identity."

"Have ye asked your husband for help?"

Amelia snorted. "No, we rarely do much but fight. I doubt he would care." Amelia wanted to cry with that admission.

"Lass, I think ye underestimate your husband."

Amelia shrugged and changed the subject. "I need to know if you ken anything of significance in this box?" She gently opened the box in front of Morag.

"Och, what pretty things I see within."

"My ma kept this for me and when she died, I inherited it. She told me her kin lived in the Highlands, but I was to show no one else."

"Could be she was protecting a secret only she would ken."

"I have tried making discreet inquiries over the years, but it goes nowhere. Do you ken the design on the plaid and the brooch? Do you ken which Highland clan these may belong to?"

Morag studied the items. "I ken not the design. Though it looks familiar, there are many that are similar. I see the inscription on the brooch tis Latin. There is someone who may ken where the brooch was made."

"Who?" Amelia asked eagerly.

"Go to the village early on the morrow. There is a vendor there by the bakery, he sells brooches. See if he has anything similar. Ye can ask discreetly, then."

Amelia was so grateful.

"And Amelia, lass, ye *must* go first thing in the morning and at no other time, for there you will find what it is you seek," Morag said with that distant look in her eyes.

Amelia hugged her and bounded out the door. She headed to her healer's cottage. Once inside, she lit a fire, warmed some water from the barrel outside, and washed, then prepared for bed. She felt lighter than she had in days; she was not alone. As long as she had kin somewhere out there; she was definitely not alone. Amelia kept rubbing the brooch in her fingers, staring at the fire. First thing in the morning, she would go to the village and begin her search.

BACK AT THE KEEP, BEISTE could not sleep. He tossed and turned in his big empty bed and felt he needed to speak to his wife and set this trouble between them to rights. Brodie and Dalziel had given him a dressing down over his move with Elora, but he did not need it. He berated himself. Getting rid of Elora had been harder to do. She had taken his actions as confirmation she would be installed as his mistress. He kicked himself hard mentally for creating more trouble for himself.

Beiste had not seen Amelia after dinner, nor did she return to her chambers. He figured she'd be there by now, though; it was getting closer to midnight, and he knew she had retainers with her, so he was not concerned. Finally, he checked on her.

He walked past the guard stationed at her door. When he touched the door handle and noticed it was not locked, he thought it was a good sign. He was willing to be rational and work things out calmly. He would even apologize for his behavior. But when Beiste opened the door to find only Orla sitting there sharpening an arrowhead, he lost his mind.

When he got hold of that wife of his, he would wring her neck!

Soon, the Keep was in an uproar. Beiste was angry and fearful. He had given Orla an earful for her perfidy and the guardsmen for being so easily tricked. Orla said she was not sure where Amelia went. She was only told to keep the guards occupied. *Clever wench.* Beiste could not believe Amelia would put herself in danger, and it was all his fault. He knew it was.

After tearing the Keep apart and finding no sign of her, word arrived that smoke was coming from the healer's cottage in the woods. He should have gone there first. Beiste was moving immediately.

When Beiste arrived at the cottage, he opened the door, ready to bellow. But he stilled when he saw Amelia sleeping peacefully on the bed. Her features were serene, even blissful, and she looked so vulnerable and alone. So alone. He did not like it one bit. He notified the men and called off the search, then stripped down and joined his wife on her bed. Gads, she was lovely, and he had missed her so much he had not realized how much until the fear of something befalling terrified him.

Amelia instantly turned towards him as if seeking his heat.

He just held her. *Daft woman.* Beiste had no intention of breaking his vows but having to answer to a woman annoyed him. Until he saw her looking so forlorn. *What was his damned pride worth if he did that to her?* She wanted him to say it out loud. He would. There would be no other woman in his bed but her.

Amelia sighed, then continued to sleep. Beiste felt something in her hand. He gently pried it from her and stared at it; it was a brooch; it was ancient, and it had an inscription in Latin. He would ask her about it in the morning. In the meantime, Beiste felt at peace for the first time in days and he slept like the dead.

WHEN BEISTE WOKE UP the next morning, he wanted to yell to the rafters, because his wife was gone. Her side of the bed was cold, meaning she had left some time ago. Damn it! *How hard was it to keep his woman in one place?* When he found her, he would wring her neck.

AMELIA LEFT EARLY THAT morning to go to the village. It surprised her to see Beiste lying beside her, but she also felt good being in his arms again. Maybe this was a temporary truce, she was not sure, but she was not sticking around to find out. Besides, she did not want to miss the brooch vendor at the village. Amelia quietly washed and dressed, then headed out the door.

Dalziel approached and told her he had assigned two guardsmen to follow her for the day, Kieran and Ranalf. Amelia had already seen them trailing not far behind her. She wanted to see how Orla fared, but she did not want to miss the vendor, so she just accepted everything else would have to wait. She told Dalziel she was headed to the village, then went to the stables to retrieve her horse.

Malise Smith

AMELIA WAS STROLLING through the village, looking over brooches in the stall. She had spoken to the vendor, but he claimed he had never seen the likeness. Feeling disappointed, she kept walking. Her guards remained close, and that was when she saw him. There was a man who looked so familiar to her, but she knew she had never met him before. When he saw her, he stopped and just stared as is if he had seen a ghost.

Amelia smiled and waved, and he waved back. She was not sure what it was, but something compelled her to make his acquaintance and she walked towards him. The man wore peasant garb over a brown and white tunic and manned a stall of pottery. He was huge, with ebony hair and specks of grey. He had a friendly smile.

She walked over to him and asked, "Have we met before? You look familiar?"

"I think the same of you too," he replied.

Amelia noticed her guards standing a scant distance away, and the stranger seemed to note them.

"Where are you from?" she asked.

"I am from the *Hebrides*," he replied.

"Oh, I have never ventured there before. What is it like?" Amelia was so excited to hear about far-off places she had never been.

"It is one of the bonniest places in the world."

"Why are you so far from home?" Amelia asked.

"I trade some of our wares." He pointed at pots and clay jars. Amelia looked at him again, but for a potter, he did not fit the profile. His hands did not look like he worked with clay, and his demeanor was regal. She thought he looked more a warrior than a merchant.

"Well, these are lovely pots. May I buy some from you?" she asked.

"But of course," he replied.

Amelia selected five small pots for some herbs and paid him. He tried to refuse the money, but she would not hear of it. Ranalf stepped forward and took them from her to carry.

"May I ask where ye are from, lass?" he asked.

"She is not a lass! She is the mistress of MacGregor Keep and newlywed to our chieftain," Kieran answered on her behalf.

Amelia was annoyed with his interference and snapped, "Thank you, Kieran, *she* can answer for herself, you ken? Now please move away." She made a shooing motion with her hand. Kieran snorted and ignored her.

"So, the Beast has wed and such a bonnie bride at that."

Amelia grinned.

"Where were you from previously?" he asked.

"I was from Dunbar."

"Ah, a lowlander, that is East Lothian way. I have heard tis lovely there by the sea and the *River Tyne*."

Amelia felt homesick then and was excited to meet someone who seemed to know the area. "Aye, tis beautiful. I miss the forest especially but tis not as pretty as the Highlands. We rode through many majestic places to get here, and I am still in awe."

"I agree with you there, Mistress. If you dinnae mind me asking, are *all* your kin in Dunbar?"

Before Amelia could answer, a familiar voice boomed from behind her, saying, "Who is asking?"

Amelia rolled her eyes, which the stranger caught, then she said, "Hello, Husband I was just talking to—"

Beiste did not let her finish before he moved her around his back and faced off with the potter.

"Beiste! Dinnae be so rude," Amelia hissed.

They looked to be of similar size, and the potter did not cower.

"Greetings Chieftain. I am Malise... Smith. Good to meet you."

"Why are you asking my wife questions about her kin?" Beiste demanded.

By this stage, Amelia had forced her way around Beiste and was trying to nudge him out of the way with her elbow and hips, which was like trying to move a boulder.

"Husband! I was talking to him first," she growled.

Beiste just rolled his eyes, and Malise smirked.

"I meant no harm. Your wife looked familiar to me and I thought to converse," Malise replied.

Realizing she was getting nowhere, Amelia tried to salvage what politeness she could. "Well, twas lovely to meet you, Mr. Smith. I am Amelia and I hope mayhap we could talk about the *Hebrides* if we meet again?"

Beiste glared down at her and growled.

"Or not," Amelia added.

"Good day, sir," Beiste said. He clasped Amelia's hand and started walking away.

Malise bade farewell and Amelia smiled and waved as she was being dragged away, unruffled by her husband's gruffness.

Malise just chuckled and waved back.

Beiste did not enjoy seeing his wife chatting so animatedly with that man. There was a familiarity between them he did not like. It grated on his nerves that he was jealous of a man who could be closer to his father's age. He needed to get a grip on his emotions, but he had missed Amelia, even with her ranting at him and trying to nudge him away. Any interaction she gave him was a boon, and he never wanted to see her disappear into her shell again. He loved that about her. *Love?* When did that word come into his thoughts? He did not want to ponder it too much.

When they made their way back through the village, Amelia felt so happy, and she did not know why. The meeting with the brooch vendor had been a disappointment, but meeting Malise had raised her spirits somehow and then to have Beiste interacting with her, albeit in his usual overbearing manner, felt good. The coldness had vanished between them and for however long it lasted, she would enjoy it.

That night Beiste and Amelia were back to sleeping in the same chambers and he made love to her for hours with a ferocity that even surprised himself. He only needed to touch her, and he was ready to explode. For his efforts, Amelia rewarded him by shouting his name several times in pleasure.

Amelia felt sated and replete as she was drifting off to sleep when Beiste said, "I am sorry Amie for everything. I have not and will never break my vows to you."

There it was, hard-fought and won but given, nonetheless.

"And I have not and will never break my vows to you," Amelia promised in return.

Chapter 14

Running a Keep

In the morning, it surprised Amelia to find Beiste still curled up beside her and he was in no hurry to leave. They got ready together and breakfasted together in the privacy of their chambers and Beiste did something he had never done before; he discussed his plans for the day with Amelia, so she knew where he was if she needed him.

The first order of the day was to show Amelia around the Keep. Beiste decided it was high time she took over as chatelaine, which was remiss of him. She had been there a month already and although she knew many people; it was Beiste's responsibility to ensure that everyone respected the authority of his wife; it was time the Keep staff took orders from her and no other.

It was the first time Amelia had been given a tour of the entire Keep. The storeroom and water cisterns were in the basement level, the kitchen and stables, as she knew, were on ground level. The Great Hall she had seen several times and the chapel, but she had never seen all the private chambers on the floor above. There was also a top floor which Beiste seemed reluctant to go, so she let that wait for another day. She knew the whereabouts of the privies, the staircases she used daily, and found out they could be removed during an attack. But the highlight was when Beiste took her to the tower. The view was breathtaking, and she could see the whole shire from there.

Beiste also introduced Amelia to Wallace Duncan, who monitored the books and household expenditure and Deidre the acting chatelaine.

When notified that Amelia would take over, Deidre's face soured slightly, but she agreed.

Wallace Duncan appeared to take issue with Amelia. He seemed nervous and talked down to her as if she were unlearned. He paid her polite attention if Beiste was around and was subtly condescending towards her when her husband was absent.

Amelia was introduced to serfs, crofters, farmers, tradespeople, skilled laborers, blacksmiths, and all the staff who kept the entire elaborate Keep system running.

Amelia also learned how busy her husband was, including Dalziel and Brodie. The three of them oversaw the security, building maintenance, Keep construction, crop rotation and farmers, tenants, and crofters' homes. They also organized trade deals with other clans, dealt with correspondence from kings and courtiers, and maintained the high level of training of their men.

One day a month, Beiste held a court of Petty Sessions where he would attempt to settle local grievances from any clan members, and he also called special council meetings with regional representatives.

Having a better understanding of how the entire system worked, Amelia was determined to do her part to help her husband lead in the manner expected of him. She was so busy she rarely had time for leisure. But the work excited her. She had a purpose. Never one to be idle, she dove headfirst into Keep matters and still made time to teach Sorcha, maintain her gardens and spend a little time with Jonet.

Orla proved to be a godsend. Her knowledge of the entire estate and observations of the people in it were priceless information. She soon transitioned from lady's maid to Amelia's most trusted advisor and friend. A relationship the two women treasured.

The biggest change was in the relationship between Amelia and Beiste. The more he let her in, the better they worked together. Their days were busy and their nights passionate. Gone was the discord between them as they presented a united front to the clan.

Cracks

AFTER A FORTNIGHT OF managing the household, Amelia noticed slight cracks in the way things ran in the Keep. Beth, the cook, was not getting the salt she constantly requested, but felt she could not complain because she had been told there were not enough funds for seasoning food.

Marvin the beekeeper still had not received payment for the candle wax he had sent to the Keep weeks ago and he needed those funds to maintain his livelihood. The seamstress had requested extra staff to help with the garment orders for winter, but no extra staff were assigned, and so it went on.

The baker could not bake the amount of bread he would otherwise produce because one oven was still in need of repairs and as Amelia talked to staff throughout the Keep, they were complaining about all the little things they needed to do their task well, but which were not provided. They had tried to go to Beiste, but Wallace Duncan had strict instructions no one was to bother the chieftain.

That afternoon, Amelia slipped into the study where the estate books were kept. She knew Beiste was away hearing Petty Session grievances and Wallace Duncan had gone to the village on an estate matter. As she studied the ledgers, according to the notes, the beekeeper had not delivered the candle wax on time and so there was no pay. Salt was supplied to the kitchens with a bill of sale attached; the oven had been repaired with a bill for repairs, staff had been assigned to the seamstress and their wages paid.

But Amelia had seen for herself that the candle wax had been delivered. The kitchens had not received the costly salt it ordered. The oven was still damaged, and the seamstress was indeed working interminable nights alone. She noted the initials DW York was written against all the payments for items and services rendered and as she poured through the ledgers, the same name kept appearing over several months.

Amelia wondered who this person was who could offer such a variety of services. She would ask Beiste when he returned and confess she could read.

As she was about to walk out of the study, she heard a noise that seemed unusual to her, and she paused. It came from inside the room, a muffled sound from behind the wall. It sounded like someone was in distress.

Amelia walked to the wall and put her ear against it. She heard a man talking to a woman, and they were arguing. Then the voices became muffled and seemed to drift away.

Amelia walked out of the study and looked about to see if there was another room close by, but there was nothing but a stone wall. Yet the talking sounded like it came from inside the wall. She asked Lachlan and Fergus, her guards for the day, "Do either of you ken if there is a room behind these walls? I thought I heard voices."

Fergus answered, "No mistress, but these Keeps echo a lot. Tis just voices carrying in the wind."

Puzzled, she decided it was another thing she would have to ask Beiste later.

That evening Amelia held off, telling Beiste about the ledgers until she had studied it some more. But she asked Beiste about hearing voices within the walls. He just shrugged and told her sound often traveled through the Keep and it might have been just coming from the floor below.

THE MAN IN THE SHADOWS stood quietly, staring at the naked woman before him. She was exquisite, and she always serviced him well.

She walked over to the wall, placed her hands upon it, and spread her legs, her scarred back towards him.

"What do you have to say for yourself, slave?"

"I am sorry, Master. I have failed you."

"Aye you have!" he shouted and brought the whip down upon her back. The sound of it cracking upon skin reverberated across the empty stone walls.

She winced in pain but remained standing as he flayed her again and again and again until she was crying, her back bloodied, freshly healed wounds reopened.

"Please Master, stop. What must I do?" she begged.

He dropped the whip and took time to admire his artistry of blood.

Then he leaned forward, pressed his mouth against her ear, and whispered, "Make sure she does not produce an heir."

"Aye Master, I will." The woman sobbed.

He walked away as she collapsed onto the icy stone floor.

The Council

IT WAS A RARE SUNNY day, and Amelia worked in her herb garden. Beiste joined her for an hour because he missed seeing her during the day.

It was while she was potting some seeds she asked, "Beiste, what do the council do?" He had mentioned he would call a council meeting soon.

"They are shire representatives, and we decide about the village or any matters that concern the MacGregors."

"Who is on the council?"

"Well, there's me, Marcus Baird and Leon Snipes the councilmen of the village, Brodie, Dalziel, Shaun Douglas represents the old guard, Abbot Hendry the church, Eoin Murray the farmers and tenants,

Gordon Buchanan the builders and guild tradesmen and Wallace Duncan the Keep staff. Hendry and Leon also speak several languages, so they can translate when we get any missives we cannot read."

"Husband, why are there no women on this council?" Amelia asked.

"What do you mean? There's never been a need for women before."

Amelia frowned. "Well, if you mean to discuss matters dealing with the MacGregors, are women not part of our clan?"

Beiste knew where Amelia was going with this, but he was more heartened that she referred to his clan as 'our', meaning she had accepted her place in it. "Aye, but usually, they answer to a man in their family who will represent them."

Amelia paused from putting dirt in pots and gave her husband a quelling look. "Beiste MacGregor, how many men would ken a woman's needs better than a woman?"

Beiste grinned. "Aye minx, I fathom your point. Women are absurd creatures, and no man ever kens what they want."

Amelia glared at him with an expression that illustrated she wanted to throw a pot at his head. Beiste stifled a laugh and asked, "So, what are ye suggesting?"

"Well, seeing as I am running the domestic side of things, mayhap I should be present at these meetings and bring a woman's thinking to the table?"

"Would you like to come with me to the next meeting?" he asked.

She beamed. "Really? I would love to husband. I promise not to talk too much. I'll just listen. You will not even ken I'm there."

And so it was that Amelia was brimming with excitement to join her first council meeting. She talked about it incessantly all week, to Orla and Sorcha and Jonet and Kieran and Beth in the kitchens, Marvin the beekeeper, Donald her guard, and Harlow the baker. Such was her excitement at being included in a grand council meeting.

However, when the day of the meeting finally arrived, within twenty minutes of the first order of business being discussed, that is a MacGregor cow mating with a Buchanan prized bull, Amelia fell asleep. According to Beiste she then snored throughout the rest of the meeting, much to the amusement of the council.

It was after the meeting and Beiste was carrying Amelia to their chambers. He could tell she was exhausted when she said, "Husband mayhap you can invite me to join in when there is a matter of real importance to discuss."

He feigned outrage. "What do you mean? All men's matters are important."

She rolled her eyes. "A cow and a bull? Really husband?" He chuckled when she said, "I dinnae have time for such wee matters. I am a very busy and important woman, you ken?" She yawned and rested her head on his shoulder.

Beiste noticed Amelia was becoming worn out by the afternoons he had decided she needed to take rest. He did not want her to become sick or overtired.

Chapter 15

Duart Castle, Isle of Mull, Hebrides

Chieftain Gilleain Maclean, otherwise known as 'Battle-Axe', sat around the table with his sons Bristi, Gillebride, and Malise, trying to process what Malise was telling him.

"Da, this Amelia lass is the spitting image of our sister when she was younger. She even has one green eye and one brown and the same-colored hair, and for her to be named Ma's middle name, it canna all be a coincidence."

Gilleain asked, "Where does she hail from?"

"The Dunbar clan in East Lothian."

"How is she on MacGregor land?" asked Bristi.

"She is married to their chieftain, the Beast."

Gilleain stiffened, disturbed by the news. "I have heard of the Beast. They say he cuts down men in his swathe like a berserker."

"They say the same of you with your battle-axe," Gillebride said with pride.

"Does she look well? He has not harmed her? Men can be brutal off the battlefield," Gilleain asked, bracing for the answer.

"No, Da, she looks hale. He is very gentle with her, for one so menacing, and she defies him. She does not fear him at all, and more puzzling, he does not seem to mind."

The men all seemed to relax with that response, and Gilleain looked proud. A light came into his eyes as he chuckled. "Aye, she must be related for certain, that defiance can only come from our clanswomen."

They all agreed.

"You remember how your ma was whenever I scowled at her? Even if I were standing three feet away fresh from battle wielding my battle-axe and shouting, the daft woman would just screech right back at me to stop tracking mud all over her clean floors!"

All four of them burst out laughing at the memory.

"Ma could stand up to you something fierce when she was riled and so could our sister," Gillebride replied.

The four of them became sombre once more.

"Aye, and I loved her for it. Like *màthair,* like daughter," Gilleain rasped as his throat clogged up with the memories.

The men become sullen, recalling another time when they held the joy of the world in their hands.

"This Amelia, Da, when she smiles, she reminds me of Ma, God rest her soul."

Gilleain bowed his head in contemplation. He did not know this lass, but he already felt an affinity towards her. Could he hope she was his granddaughter? Would he finally find out what happened to his daughter?

"Have ye spoken with her?"

"I have, and she has the same kind nature as our sister. I tried to speak more, but the Beast warned me off several times."

"Do they ken who you are?"

"No, I used a false last name. I was pretending to be a potter, remember? I will say, though, the Beast is very protective of her."

"Da," Bristi said, "we have searched for many years. I think it wise to find out more of this, Amelia. If she is our niece, then she belongs with us."

"True, we have spent too many years with loss. It would be good to gain something for a change." A sheen of unshed tears watered

Gilleain's eyes. The room fell into silence as if the grief of losing a daughter and sister still hung over them.

Gilleain cleared his throat. "What of the MacGregor? What do ye make of him?"

"He is wise from the talk of the locals. They say his father supported Duncan, but Beiste's position is unclear, which is why Macbeth has tried to make peace through this marriage."

"So, Macbeth favors the Beast, and the Beast favors his wife."

Gilleain was contemplative, rubbing his beard with his thumb and index finger. "If she is kin, I need to ken how she ended up a Dunbar."

Malise replied, "I already sent a man to *Belhaven* two sennights ago to ask discreetly about her and I've left one of our men at *Glenorchy* to keep watch from a distance. We should have word soon."

HOURS LATER, GILLEAIN of the Battle Axe was well into his cups and going over again all the heartache and loss he had suffered over the years. Not only losing his beloved wife, Moira-Amelia but also his only daughter. *That silly chit. She was his favorite child.* After his wife's death, he sent her to the abbey, but when she learned he had signed betrothal contracts for her to marry a Norseman; she ran away. They searched for years but he never heard from her again and it broke his heart.

Gilleain decided if this Amelia was his granddaughter, then nothing and no one would keep him from her. She belonged in *Mull* with her kin, and he would even battle the Beast himself for her.

With that thought and a firm determination set in his mind, he took another large swig of his whiskey, and as it burned down his throat, he stood on unsteady feet and stared at the crossed battle axes hanging over the wall. He beat his chest and roared the clan motto inscribed over the fireplace — *Either Conquer or Die.*

FIVE DAYS LATER A MESSAGE arrived at Duart Castle. Amelia MacGregor was the illegitimate daughter of the Earl of Dunbar and a woman called Iona who had died seven years prior.

Upon hearing the news, Gilleain and his sons wept bittersweet tears at the loss of a daughter and sister, Iona-Moira Maclean, and at the joyful discovery of a granddaughter and niece. They immediately sent a missive to *Glenorchy*. The content was brief. *"The Macleans are coming to claim their kin."*

Chapter 16

MacGregor Keep, Glenorchy

"Are you looking for me?" Amelia asked, as Deidre stood in the open doorway of her private bedchamber.

"Aye, Mistress, I was wondering why ye are working here in this cramped room when you could be in the solar above," Deidre asked.

Amelia shrugged. "I suppose I just assumed they were not to be used as my husband has not shown me around up there."

"Mistress, anyone can use them. They just have not had the opportunity yet. Come, tis lovely up there." Deidre gestured for Amelia to follow her.

Amelia ascended the stairs to the top floor. Her guardsman for the day, Donald ambled behind her. Once on the top floor, Amelia felt a slight reluctance to venture further.

"I'm not sure I should be in here," Amelia said.

Deidre assured her. "You are the new mistress, and you should put your touches on the place."

Amelia had to admit it was lovely, if a little dusty. "Tis so lovely here, and the sunshine is far better here than the dark rooms."

"Aye Mistress, tis pleasant during the wintry days."

"I should check with Beiste first." Amelia wanted his approval before changing things around.

"Why? The chieftain will not want you bothering him about rooms he assumes you will use. He has enough decisions to make these days," Deidre replied.

After some internal struggle, Amelia had to agree these rooms would make an excellent solar, drawing room, and sewing room.

Deidre left her, saying she would return with some extra hands to help. Donald stood guard by the stairway as Amelia got busy clearing out rooms that looked as if they had not seen a good dusting in years.

Memories and Dust

HOURS PASSED, AND THE light was fading, but Amelia felt rejuvenated for having cleaned out two rooms. She hung bright tapestries along the walls; the fire was roaring, and the room looked warmer and more inviting. She was thinking of asking Beiste for some furniture so she could create a suitable Drawing Room where she could hold her meetings during the day.

She noticed the women Deidre promised to help never arrived, but Amelia did not mind working on her own, as she was used to it. Feeling industrious, she kept going between rooms, dusting, and cleaning.

Amelia was rummaging through an old chest in the corner of one room when she found the most exquisite handmade baby boots. She rummaged further and found an embroidered blanket for a bairn. *There was a bairn in this room? Why was it empty now and where was the bairn?*

She heard footsteps drawing near and turned to see Orla running and panting, catching her breath as if she had run miles. "Amelia, what are ye doing here? You must come away now, tis not good to be here."

"Why, what do you mean? Tis a beautiful room."

"No, Mistress, it's not that, tis the chieftain's late wife's room."

"I ken it. Deidre told me to get a start. She was coming to help soon."

Orla was panicking already and grabbing Amelia by the arm.

"What is the matter, Orla?" Amelia felt slightly uneasy now.

"Deidre has deceived you, she, and that Elora bitch. They mean you harm by having you here!"

"What do you mean?" Amelia was following Orla.

"Those evil witches had me sent off on a fools' errand, or I would have stopped you sooner."

Orla looked around and saw all the changes. She crossed herself. "Oh, lud you have made too many changes, he will not be happy."

Then the realization hit Amelia. "Oh bollocks, Beiste doesna let anyone in here, does he?"

"No." Orla shook her head. "It has been locked up and forbidden for any of the women to come here or make any changes."

"This is a shrine to his late wife."

Orla just nodded.

"He must have loved her a great deal. What have I done?" Amelia looked around the room at all the changes she had made.

Orla paused. "Mayhap we can go downstairs and explain it to him before he kens."

Before they could make good on their decision, the door was flung wide and Beiste stood in the doorway, glaring at them.

"What the devil do you think you're doing here?" he demanded.

It filled Beiste with rage that this was the one place he did not want tainting, his new bride. Yet there she was in all her vibrancy, mired in the darkness that represented his failings and loss.

"I am sorry, Husband, Deidre said I could use this room," Amelia replied.

"No one is to use this part of the Keep. Do you hear me? No one! Not even you. Leave now!"

Beiste was clenching his fists and breathing heavily. Already, the memories of all he had lost came flooding back. His eyes were glazed, as if he was somewhere else.

Amelia replied, "All right, Beiste."

She grabbed Orla's arm, and they made their way towards the door. As she passed Beiste, his body still rigid, she paused, stood on tiptoe, and brushed her lips against his cheek. Then she whispered, "I'm very sorry, Husband, I did not mean to disrespect the memory of your late wife. Forgive me." Amelia hugged him around his middle, then made to walk away, but not before Beiste dragged her back, kissed her forehead, and let her go.

Amelia squeezed his arm, then left the room.

Beiste instantly calmed. *Trust his wife to placate him with such tenderness.* The darkness receded with her soft touch, and she soothed his soul. Beiste remained standing in a room he promised he would never enter again. For the first time, he saw it in a unique light. He looked around and was greeted with color and vibrancy and life.

He saw a tapestry hanging on the wall, woolen throws over sparse furnishings. The rooms were dusted and cleaned, and the fireplace cleared of ash. It now had neatly laid firewood in the grate and fragrant flowers in containers distributed about the room. The scent of lavender and forest replaced what was once dark, dank mold. His wee wife had wrought such obvious changes.

Beiste walked into the adjoining room that was to be a nursery. There was a chest he knew was still full of the clothes Caitrin had been sewing for their bairn. The chest was still open, Amelia must have been looking through it. He saw the white baby garments and tiny blanket. There was a large rug on the floor, which made it seem warm and welcoming. He remembered happier times in this room when he placed his hand on Caitrin's tummy and the babe had moved.

Beiste looked out the window and whispered to the sky, "I am sorry, Caitrin. I was not there for you and our bairn; I did not protect you as I should. I hope you have both found peace."

He felt a soft breeze pass by and the scent of lilies waft through. It was her favorite flower. Something unlocked and released deep inside him. Beiste placed the garments back inside and closed the chest. He walked back out the way he came, except this time the darkness did not consume him as it had in the past.

AFTER A THOROUGH BATH to wash off the dirt of the day, Amelia made her way to the Great Hall. She would not cower in her room but face her problems head-on. Deidre had done this deliberately, hoping to drive a wedge between her and Beiste. She would show that nothing had affected her in the least. She just hoped her husband was not too angry with her.

Amelia looked around, trying to find a sign of Deidre and Elora. They were noticeably absent. Then Sorcha appeared and made her way to the table and sat beside her. Brodie constantly scowled at Ranalf and Orla and had stopped flirting with one of the serving girls. Jonet was still eating some weird gruel.

Beiste had not appeared after half an hour had passed, but she saw Deidre and Elora enter the hall. The two women were smirking, and they gave her a smug look. She just stared them both down until they looked away.

The occupants in the hall all went quiet, and she knew Beiste must have entered. The Keep would have heard about what she had done with Caitrin's rooms, but she would brace and deal.

Beiste strolled into the hall with nonchalance.

Amelia was so relieved to see him all she could do was bid him welcome. "Welcome, Husband, tis glad I am to see you."

Beiste stood in front of her and said nothing. The hall collectively held its breath. Amelia braced herself for whatever he would unleash when he leaned down and kissed her soundly on the lips in front of the whole Keep. He then sat beside her, pulled her chair with her still on it, closer to his, and started serving his food. Whatever had darkened his mood earlier was gone.

Amelia immediately started fussing over him, filling his trencher, and making sure her man got fed and he appeared to lavish attention.

The hall let out a collective sigh of relief, and boisterous discussion resumed.

The only two people who were not happy were Deidre and Elora.

IT WAS LATER IN THE evening Amelia lay naked on top of Beiste's chest after a strenuous round of lovemaking. Her head was tucked under his chin, his hand caressing her back, and they spoke in hushed tones. She apologized for invading Caitrin's rooms and explained how Deidre made her believe it was to be used.

"Love, tis all right. Use the rooms you are now, my wife. I think it would be good to have life breathed back in there again."

"Thank you, I ken you loved her very much and I would never presume to take her place—"

Beiste placed his finger on her lips to stop Amelia from speaking. He took a deep breath and felt it was time to share.

"Caitrin and I were not a love match, but when she discovered she was with child, twas a joyous time for both of us."

"What happened?"

"A few months later, I went to stop a skirmish with the neighboring clans. Caitrin begged me not to go. She was terrified something would happen, but I assured her she would be safe."

He paused and stared at the ceiling.

"Tell me, Husband," Amelia whispered.

"I had been gone only three days, but upon my return, I was told she had miscarried and died during the night."

Amelia took in a sharp breath.

"Turns out she bled to death, trying to abort the bairn. They found pennyroyal by her bedside," Beiste said.

Amelia hugged her husband tighter. "Oh, Beiste, tis so tragic. I am sorry for your loss."

"My uncle, Ludan, was with us during that time, and he said sometimes women who are carrying just do unexpected things. But I vowed never to use those rooms again."

"What was she like, Beiste?"

"Scared. She was always scared if I went away, she would fret until I returned."

"Do you ken what it was she feared?"

"No, she had guards, all the time to keep her safe, and I was usually close by, but when she became pregnant, her fear increased. I should have kept a closer vigil over her, and for that, I failed."

"Husband, you cannot blame yourself for things not under your control."

Beiste kissed the top of her head. "Aye."

"Thank you for sharing with me."

Beiste pulled the covers up over them. "Tis time to sleep, Love."

Amelia had to agree as she drifted off to sleep, feeling safe in Beiste's arms.

Trouble

IT WAS SEVERAL DAYS later, around midday, and Beiste had returned to their bedchamber to change into a fresh leine. When he entered the room, he found Elora lying naked in the bed, beckoning to him.

He scowled and yelled, "Get out!"

"Surely you dinnae mean that?" She pouted.

"I do, now get out. How dare you sully our bed?"

With desperation and knowing she was losing the battle, Elora stood up and walked seductively towards him naked. "I offer you the use of my body to do as you please, and I expect nothing in return. Surely you cannot be satisfied with just one woman?" Elora asked.

Beiste was not even tempted. There was a time the mere sight of a naked woman in his bed was enough to make him drive into her with abandon. Not anymore.

Beiste replied, "You will leave my chambers now and never come back." With that, he picked up her robe, wrapped it around her, and pushed her out the door despite her protests. He then slammed it shut and went back to getting his leine.

Amelia came to a sudden stop in the hallway as she gawked at a half-naked Elora getting pushed out of their bedchamber.

Elora turned and stared her straight in the face. She then smiled and sashayed past Amelia, straightening her robe. As Elora passed her, she said, "You may go to him, he has at least relieved some of his stress inside me, he will be much gentler with you now." She strutted down the stairs with a smirk.

Standing on the top landing, looking down as Elora descended the stairs, Amelia was fuming. A million emotions raced through her system, but the prominent one was anger. She picked up a nearby container of flowers that were sitting on the ledge, took them out and tipped the dirty water over Elora's head then threw the dead flowers at her. Elora shrieked and started running down the stairs.

Amelia stormed down the hall to her own chamber and slammed the door, locking it behind her. She began packing her belongings and setting plans in motion. *When was she going to bloody learn that men were unreliable?*

A moment later Beiste walked out of their shared chambers freshly changed and headed back to the hall where he was looking forward to joining his wife for the noonday meal.

Meanwhile, Amelia continued to stomp about her room and rant about unfaithful husbands and their harems. *Fine, if Elora is the woman Beiste desired then he could have her,* she thought. She was not about to slink off and lick her wounds in some backwater shire. She belonged here now. She was Chieftain MacGregor's wife. He had promised her a home, and this was it but there was no way she would remain anywhere near his blasted chambers and witness women coming and going all hours. No, she was going to permanently move to the healer's cottage where she could live out her days as an independent woman.

Misunderstandings

BEISTE WAITED FOR HIS wife in the hall and she did not show for the noon meal. He was becoming impatient, wondering if he should just go in search of her when the woman in question appeared, her head held high, defiance and anger shining in her eyes. He watched as she started dragging an enormous trunk of clothes down the stairs. He stood and walked across the hall to help her, but she smacked his hands away. "Dinnae touch my things," Amelia scolded.

"What in bloody hell are you doing? You cannot carry that, tis too heavy. Where are you taking it?"

"Where I move my things tis none of your concern any longer, Beiste."

Amelia spotted Kieran passing the stairway and called out, "Kieran would you be so kind as to help me carry this chest?" She gave him a winning smile.

"Of course, Mistress I'd be glad to help."

Kieran bent to lift it and Beiste slammed his foot down on it. "Leave it," he growled.

Kieran backed away.

"Kieran, please ignore my husband." Amelia turned to Beiste and said, "Move your damn foot!"

"No."

She physically tried to wrestle his leg, but it would not budge. "Oh, you big-footed monster. Move your foot!" she shouted.

"Not until you tell me what's going on?" Beiste replied.

Amelia turned back to Kieran with all politeness and asked, "Kieran would you kindly help me move the chieftain's foot off my trunk?"

Beiste snarled, "Kieran if you take a step closer, I will geld you!"

Kieran looked between the two of them. "I think mayhap I should come back later when you two have discussed your foot." He started walking backward away from them.

"Coward!" Amelia yelled.

"I'm sorry, Mistress, but I treasure my balls too much to get in the middle of this," Kieran replied.

"Next time you get stabbed with a knife I'll leave you to bleed to death on the roadside and poison your food and smother you with honey and let the ants eat you alive and let Morag see to you instead," Amelia ranted at his retreating figure.

Kieran chuckled but kept walking away. "I'll keep that in mind, Mistress."

Beiste was trying hard not to grin at Amelia's tirade because once she got going, she would not stop.

"Now wife, what is all this about? What has you so riled?"

"I am moving to the healer's cottage permanently."

"Why?"

"You have been carrying on with Elora behind my back..."

"What? When?"

"Dinnae lie to me, Husband, or I swear I will punch you in the mouth and give you a matching scar on the other side," Amelia said with her fist clenched.

"What the bloody hell do you mean you infuriating woman?"

"I saw Elora come out of our chambers half-naked," she hissed trying to keep her voice down because everyone in the hall was straining to hear the conversation. Even Beth the cook had stopped midway to the kitchens bending an ear towards them.

"Mind your own work, Beth!" Amelia yelled.

Beth looked startled then huffed and kept walking, muttering, "I wasn't even listening."

Beiste said, "Nothing happened, Love. I told you I will never break my vows. I gave you my word."

"But Husband tis hard to believe when she is attractive." Amelia looked downcast.

"And you are not?" He looked at her incredulously. "Amie, Sweeting, she was lying in my bed naked when I got to the chambers, and I set her outside the door."

"But she said that you two had rutted together."

"She said what? She lied. I will not stand for it!" Beiste looked outraged. He removed his foot off her trunk and stormed out the hall entrance.

Amelia realized then he was serious, and she chased after him. "All right, Husband, I believe you. I believe you, I'm sorry... mayhap you need to calm down." She knew what he was like when he got this way.

"I will not calm down when someone spreads lies about me," Beiste growled.

They made their way to Elora's home only to hear moans coming from within. Beiste did not care he banged on the door once and yelled, "I'm coming in!" Then he kicked the door open.

It was just in time to see a naked Lachlan standing with his head thrown back, both hands holding the head of a scantily clad Elora who was kneeling on the floor, pleasuring him with her mouth.

She screeched and they separated immediately trying to cover themselves.

Amelia despite her curiosity blushed and covered her eyes having seen far more than she ever wanted to see.

Without missing a beat Beiste boomed, "Dinnae lie to my wife ever again Elora and if I ever find you naked in my bed uninvited, I will throw you in the dungeons you hear me?"

Elora was hiding behind Lachlan and nodded.

Amelia felt sorry for the woman, so she said, "Beiste mayhap tis, not the best time."

He turned and glared at her. She shut her mouth.

"You waited in the chieftain's bed naked? Kenning he's already married?" Lachlan yelled at Elora.

"Lachie, darling..." Elora tried to soothe him.

"You tried to seduce the chieftain and then came to me?" Lachlan looked genuinely hurt. "I just asked you to marry me, Elora."

"Honey, please I was all pent up and needed release you ken how it is," Elora pleaded.

Amelia felt increasingly uncomfortable being party to a conversation that should be private.

Beiste interrupted them and said, "Lachlan word of advice, keep your trews on around that woman."

Beiste clasped Amelia's hand and dragged her out the door. He was furious and walking so fast she was struggling to keep pace.

"Husband."

"Quiet!"

She opened her mouth to speak, and Beiste said, "Quiet!"

"You are walking too fast I cannot keep up."

Beiste stopped and swung her up into his arms, then kept walking. She held on.

"I am sorry, Beiste. I should have trusted you. But you should ken what it looked like. How would you like it if you saw me with a half-naked man?"

Beiste stopped walking and glared at her. "I would kill him and throw his body in the fire, then revive him and kill him again."

"Right... um, good to know, my love."

He continued his stride trying to shake the thought from his mind then he stopped again. "Never leave me. Do you hear me? If you are angry or upset you come and yell at me, you dinnae just start moving out of our chambers."

Amelia nodded. "Aye. I am sorry, Beiste."

That seemed to pacify him, and he nodded and kept walking.

"Husband."

"What?" he growled.

"Do all men have large… uh, man parts?"

He paused. "What are you talking about?"

"Well, I could not help but notice that Lachlan is rather big, and I just wondered if —"

"Stop!" Beiste growled.

Amelia looked surprised.

"Never talk to me about the size of Lachlan's man part."

"I didna say it was bigger than yours. I was just asking for healing purposes —"

"Enough Amelia. I forbid you to think about any mans' parts!"

"All right."

They continued on in silence for a while when Beiste said, "And the answer is no. They are not all big and *mine* is the only one you need to concern yourself with."

"All right, Husband." Amelia kissed his jaw. "I was just curious."

Beiste just shook his head and muttered, "Daft woman."

THE FOLLOWING MORNING Beiste woke to a pleasurable sensation between his legs. He peered down to the view of his buxom wife pleasuring his hardened length with her tongue and giving him a mischievous wink. He groaned and threw his head back, writhing in rhythm with her ministrations. When he could not take any more, he growled and in one swoop had her pinned beneath him, her legs spread apart and his head between her thighs.

She was pouting, her upper body resting on her elbows glaring down at him. "Beiste! I was trying something new."

"I appreciate it but right now I prefer the old way." With that, he began his ministrations and Amelia abandoned her argument.

Soon after Beiste was braced above her, driving deep. The sounds of their loud coupling could be heard throughout the Keep, especially when their joint climax resulted in Amelia screaming his name in ecstasy.

An hour later Amelia emerged from her bed chamber looking dazed and well and truly tumbled. As she meandered down the stairs, she had to admit she did not mind the old way either.

Chapter 17

Mysterious Plant life

It was a sunny morning and Amelia felt a little queasy and under the weather. With Orla accompanying her, she went below to the storeroom to see if she could find some ginger and peppermint to chew. It was a room she had yet to visit since Deidre had kept it under lock and key.

"I've never been down here," Orla said with excitement, as if she were going on a grand adventure.

They walked through the opening and marveled at the sheer delight of the vast expanse of stores. Amelia found some peppermint and started chewing. "Why has no one been receiving their spices and shares when this place is stocked full?"

"I am surprised as well because Cook is always complaining about not having enough stock," Orla replied.

"We better record what we find here, and I will tally it with the books."

After a while, she and Orla were rummaging through the items when Amelia came across a faint lingering odor; it reminded her of something she had smelled earlier above stairs.

Amelia moved trays and containers and jars until she found the scent and there, on the back of a shelf at the top in a dark corner, she found it, a strange plant. A vague memory warned her it was dangerous. She wondered why anyone would have this here of all places in with food supplies.

She carefully pulled out the tray, noticing a few rows were missing. It appeared someone had been using this plant, but for what purpose?

It took a few hours to catalogue stock and by then Amelia felt better chewing the ginger and mint.

When she retired upstairs, she went to her private chambers and pulled out her notebook. She scanned the sketches of plants until she found an exact match in her mother's neat drawings, including its properties. "*Datura Stramonium — Jimson Weed* a branch of nightshade — a deliriant."

Why would someone use a deliriant on purpose? The smell was so familiar; she tried to recall where she had scented it before. Amelia put her notes away and was pacing the room when the door flew open with such force it hit the wall.

She rolled her eyes. *Could the man not enter a room quietly like a normal person?*

"Are you unwell?" Beiste crossed to her straight away. "Orla said you looked slightly pale?" He started feeling her forehead. "Are ye running a fever? Have you eaten?"

"Beiste, I am fine. I just needed to clear my head."

She moved his hand away from her forehead and clasped it in hers; she kissed his knuckle. "Truly, I am all right. I was going to come to bed soon."

He visibly relaxed.

"I dinnae like it when you're not in our chambers, tis too far," he blurted out.

"Husband, I am right next door."

"I'm thinking of taking this wall down so there is no separation at all." He began walking the length of the room, working out measurements.

"Dinnae you dare, Beiste MacGregor! You'll just create unnecessary dust and rubble."

Beiste knew he was being unreasonable, but when had he been reasonable around his wife? When Orla told him Amelia was feeling unwell, he had panicked. He had gone to their room and waited patiently for a whole five minutes before the sound of her pacing bothered him. For someone who could never stomach the company of a woman before, he just could not get enough of her, and he did not care. Men could be needy, too.

"Well, come on then, wife." He dragged her out of her chambers and locked the door behind him. They walked straight into their room, and he slammed the door shut before bending down and capturing her lips with his.

After a passionate embrace, Amelia asked, "What was that for?"

Beiste replied, "That was for not arguing with me once on the way here. I ken tis a short walk, but we should celebrate milestones."

Amelia burst out laughing.

Later that night, as Amelia lay in a state of half-sleep and half-dream, it came to her, where she had smelled the Jimson weed. Jonet's morning porridge. She first smelled it the morning after the wedding and once in her evening broth. She recalled Deidre prepared her meals each day.

Amelia sat up immediately.

"What is it, Love?" Beiste was awake and alert and sitting up beside her.

"Beiste, I think Deidre is poisoning your ma."

Poison

BEISTE AND AMELIA GOT up, dressed, and went directly to Jonet's room. The guard let them pass. Beiste knocked and after no sound, they entered and checked on her.

Jonet was sound asleep, but within minutes of being in the room, Amelia smelled the Jimson weed. It was faint, but the scent lingered on a cup beside her bed. There was also a scent of 'Valerian', a sedative used for sleeping draughts.

"What is it, Love?" Beiste asked.

"Beiste, your mother has been consuming Jimson weed in her morn and evening meals and in her sleeping draughts. No wonder she is confused so often."

Beiste wanted to kill someone. Right under his roof, someone had been poisoning his mother. Making her confused. But why? What was the purpose?

Beiste immediately made his way to Deidre's quarters, Amelia held his hand and followed behind. He had already notified the guards to rouse Dalziel and Brodie. Poisoning was a heinous crime. It needed three heads to decide the punishment. When he knocked, there was no answer. He opened the door to look inside, but it was empty. *Where the devil would Deidre be at this time of night?* He thought.

Beiste put a guard at her door to notify him when she returned. All the guardsmen were on high alert to look out for Deidre through the Keep. At no point was she to approach Sorcha, Jonet, or Amelia.

An hour later, Dalziel dragged Deidre into the council room. The first thing Beiste noticed was she looked like a mess, which was highly unusual. Her hair was disheveled. It was usually tied back in a tight bun. She kept her back ramrod straight. She wore a loose-fitting dress with a shawl.

"Before you ask, I have not hurt her. I found her like this wandering around the South wing," Dalziel said, lest any councilman accused him of manhandling her.

After an hour of interrogations, Deidre insisted, she never knew Jimson weed was a deliriant, and any harm was unintentional. None of the men believed her at all, they knew she was hiding something, but Beiste wanted her gone so he banished her from MacGregor lands.

She cried and pleaded she became so hysterical, but he would not budge. The order went out that if she was spotted anywhere near the Keep; she was to be thrown in the dungeon.

Amelia set to work straight away trying to undo the effects of the Jimson weed on Jonet. She started by changing her entire diet to add more fresh produce and meat and bread and including saffron in her tea. Amelia also wanted the flavor brought back into her fare.

Jonet seemed to respond immediately to the taste of fresh oatmeal with stewed apples and a drizzle of honey. Amelia realized how remiss she was not seeing to Jonet's food earlier and she was determined to see her mother-in-law well again.

Chapter 18

Arch Enemies

It was some days after the incident with Deidre, and all seemed to have settled into a gentle ebb and flow over the Keep. Jonet was slowly regaining her appetite and faculties, and Amelia continued managing the Keep with Orla's help. The ledgers were still a mystery, but Amelia needed more time before she took the matter to Beiste.

Another addition to her schedule was taking archery lessons with the new bow Orla fashioned for her. It was at one such lesson Amelia discovered something strange between her close friend and Brodie Fletcher.

Dalziel had scheduled time for the women to use the archery range for practice down by the training grounds, and Orla had set up their session. Amelia would join her once she finished her lessons with Sorcha. It was when Amelia approached a little later that she witnessed something she had never seen before. The calm, quiet Orla was spitting mad as the usually affable Brodie raged at her.

A Gifted Bowyer

BRODIE WATCHED ORLA polishing the reed of the bow she had made for Amelia. It shone and would provide her mistress with an excellent weapon for defense and hunting. Brodie saw the intricate design and inlay for what it was: superb craftsmanship. He knew Orla was an exceptional bowyer because he had seen her work before.

Most men thought it beneath them to take weapons crafted by a woman, but the few archers he knew who had commissioned her to craft their bows swore by her skill. She knew how to craft the right specification for each man, and her arrows struck true every time.

Brodie admired Orla from a distance for as long as he could remember, but the feeling was not mutual. Her sharp tongue could flay him alive.

Brodie came closer, mesmerized, as he watched her practice. When Orla came to the training grounds, he loved it. He purposefully made sure he was around to watch as she stretched and taut the bow, imagining the direction of the target before she let her arrow fly. He saw her visibly relax and focus as her breathing slowed. Brodie watched her chest rise and fall and he had never wanted to be a bow so much in his life, to have her touch him like that. He moved even closer and realized his mistake. His shadow threw her off her focus when she had just been taking a deep breath to shoot.

Orla turned with the arrow nocked and ready to fire, but stopped when she saw it was Brodie. She scowled at him.

No woman ever looked at him like he was nothing other than God's gift. Quicker than she could think, he had disarmed her of the bow and arrow and went on the offensive.

"Well, if it isn't little Orla playing at being a hunter," Brodie said. He did not even know why he taunted her.

Then the little hoyden mimicked back, "Well, if it isn't little Brodie playing at being a man."

Brodie's smile vanished, replaced by annoyance. "Come now, Orla, you ken I am *all* man, and there is nothing *little* about me. Och, but wait, you wouldna ken because you've never had a man." He smirked.

Orla's quip was instant and biting. "And glad I am of it. Better to be untouched than riddled with the pox."

Brodie gritted his teeth and towered over her. "I dinnae have the pox."

She did not even flinch. "Sorry I didna mean you I just meant half the women you bed."

Now he was livid. "I dinnae lie with pox riddled women and I'd watch my tongue if I were you to spread such vile rumors."

Orla's hands were on her hips as she faced off with him. "Trust me, Brodie Fletcher. I dinnae talk about you at all. You're not worth the time."

Brodie clenched his fists. "Good, make sure of it... Orphan!"

She grimaced at that word then yelled, "Asshole!" Orla snatched her bow out of Brodie's hand and stormed over to Amelia who had witnessed the entire thing and looked a little shocked.

Brodie could not believe how much Orla got under his skin. She mocked him at every turn. *It was unheard of.* Women fell over themselves for his attention. There must be something wrong with Orla was the only explanation he could summon. *Touched in the head.* That would explain it. That was the last time he would think kindly of her bowyer skills.

"Are you all right Orla?" Amelia asked tentatively as Orla was seething mad.

"Aye, I'm fine. Just that bloody brute always gets in my way. Now come on, let us get started." She practically ordered.

It amused Amelia to see this bossy side of Orla. It was high time her friend stopped letting people walk all over her. Amelia made a mental note to keep a closer eye on her. She owed Orla a lot, and she would protect her in return.

The Missive from Mull

THE COUNCIL GATHERED for their regular meeting when a missive arrived. It was from the Macleans. Beiste wondered what business they would want with him. When the parchment was handed over, he paused when he saw the wax seal. He had seen that symbol before on a silver brooch his wife was holding the night, he found her in the healer's cottage. He meant to ask Amelia about it and just never got around to it.

He broke the seal, but dread and curiosity were already seeping into his veins. When he read the contents, it took him time to get his head around it, then he stood and shouted at the messenger.

The councilmen stopped their meeting as Beiste threw the letter on the table. "No. You tell your laird he is not taking my wife!" he bellowed while the messenger paled.

"What is it, Brother?" Brodie gestured for Dalziel to pick up the letter as he was seated closest.

Dalziel immediately paraphrased the contents out loud. "Chieftain Maclean from the *Hebrides* claims Amelia as his granddaughter. He's on his way from the *Isle of Mull* to retrieve her... he will petition King Macbeth for an annulment if he must."

The entire room went silent.

Dalziel said, "Brother they will not take her. We will deal with them when they arrive."

Beiste who had been standing quietly until then agreed. "Aye, I will cut down any man who tries to take my wife from me."

The Brooch and Other Misdemeanors

THAT NIGHT WHEN AMELIA returned to their chambers, the room was in disarray with drawers and chests opened, clothes were strewn about the floor and Beiste sat by the fire drinking ale. He kept staring at the flames and his mood was brooding and dark. She had not seen this side of him for a while and could only guess what had happened.

"Husband? Are you well? What is the matter?" She was instantly by his side, kneeling before him with concern.

"Where is your brooch, Amelia? I searched for it and could not find it." She opened her mouth to speak when Beiste said, "Dinnae lie to me, wife. I want to ken about your brooch."

"Aye, calm down I will show you." Amelia retrieved the oak box from the chamber next door and brought it to him. He stared at it like it held vipers. Amelia opened the box, took out the brooch, and gave it to him.

Beiste sat and studied it for some time before saying, "How long have you had this?"

"Since my ma died. She gave it to me with her belongings in that box but asked me not to show it to anyone."

"So, all this time you kenned you were a Maclean, and you never told me?" He scowled.

"A who? What are you talking about?"

Beiste took the box from her, opened it fully, and pulled out the contents.

"This is the Maclean plaid and their crest badge."

Amelia was stunned and then excited. "Really? You mean to tell me you ken which clan these belong to?" Tears instantly stained her cheeks.

"Aye, you mean you never kenned?" Beiste asked.

She shook her head. "I never kenned." Amelia was wiping her tears and said, "My ma told me on her deathbed to find my kin and give this to them so they would ken who I was, but I could never figure it out, until now. Ma failed to mention their name and her letter only mentioned the box."

Amelia held the plaid in her hands and lovingly caressed it, then looked up at Beiste. "My kin are the Macleans? Truly?"

The awe and wonder on her face was something Beiste could not ignore.

"Aye, Love, they are from the *Isle of Mull*."

Amelia looked so surprised. "They are from an isle... oh Beiste, I am sure it must be a bonnie place." She had a wistful expression on her face and it moved Beiste deeply.

She was killing him; she had no idea who her family was all these years and now they wanted her, and Beiste could not let her go.

He gentled his voice and asked, "Amie, why did you not trust me with this information?"

"I am sorry, Beiste. I just thought I'd find them myself, eventually." She shrugged her shoulders.

Beiste knew why. It was because all her life Amelia had to do everything on her own, rely only on herself. It was his job to make sure she trusted him with everything from now on.

"Husband, do you think these Macleans would want to ken me if I were to send them a message?" she asked.

That is when Beiste saw it, the vulnerability in her eyes. Amelia yearned to meet her kin, and she wanted them to accept her. Beiste took a deep breath and sighed. He reached out for her and pulled her onto his lap. He stroked her back as they both stared into the fire then he whispered, "Aye, Love, how could they not want you? You are the most precious woman on God's earth."

Amelia smiled, then she kissed him deeply. "Thank you, this is why I love you. You ken how to soothe my troubled soul." With that, she rested her head on his shoulder.

Beiste stiffened. He could not breathe. His wife just said she loved him and for some inextricable reason, it struck him with fear and elation.

Amelia did not care if Beiste knew. It was the truth she had fallen in love with her own husband, and he would just have to deal with it.

Beiste relaxed and pulled her closer. It was then he had an epiphany. He loved her too, from the moment she yelled at him on that dusty road. But he decided not to tell her that because he was a warrior, not some emasculated poet prancing about town writing love-sick sonnets. He remained silent.

Beiste decided to let the old Maclean bastard see his granddaughter. But if he tried to take Amelia from him, Beiste would kill him and hope that someday his wee wife forgave him.

"Beiste?"

"Aye, Sweeting."

"Why were you looking for my brooch today?"

"No reason. I just remembered I saw it at the cottage."

There was more silence between them before he had a thought and asked, "Amie are there any other secrets you have hidden in this oak box of yours?"

"Oh no, well um not in the box at least..."

He frowned. "What do you mean? Spit it out."

"All right, there is something else you should ken."

"Tell me," Beiste said with a warning tone. He braced for whatever chaos his little termagant was about to reign on his head.

"Beiste, do you ken a person called DW York?"

"Aye, that's Deidre. Why?"

"I think Wallace Duncan and Deidre have been stealing money from the estate."

"What?" He sat up straight. "How do you ken?"

Amelia took a deep breath and decided it was time to come clean. "I read the ledgers in your study and each time DW York appears the numbers dinnae add up. I asked Wallace a few questions about supplies and each time he gave me vague answers."

There was dead silence. Beiste lifted her off his lap and stood. He just stared at her, and one of two things came to him. First, his clever wife could read and do sums, and second, she had been snooping around his study.

Amelia wore a guilty expression, biting her bottom lip.

Beiste expelled an exasperated sigh. "Show me."

Amelia nodded, grabbed his hand, and pulled him out the door towards the study.

"THOSE CONNIVING PRICKS!" Beiste scowled. "They've been draining the estate slowly accounting for services and supplies that dinnae exist." He paced the room. "Damn it to hell! They were counting on me never finding out because Ma was too ill to keep up the books, and Wallace thought you could not read."

Beiste stormed over to Amelia while she was pondering what he was saying, picked her up, and kissed her soundly. When he put her down, he said, "Thank heavens I have a clever wife." Amelia blushed with the compliment until he added, "Even if she is nosy."

"I am not," she replied indignantly. "I was uh… dusting one day, and they fell open in front of me."

Beiste just burst out laughing.

The following day a surprised Wallace Duncan was called to the council room. He assumed he was there to advise on household purchases. He was wrong. By the end of the meeting, he was stripped of his position and belongings and escorted from the Keep with only the clothes on his back. Beiste took great pleasure in informing him it was his learned wife who detected the discrepancies in his accounting and if Wallace ever set foot on MacGregor land, he would not leave it alive.

Two days later Deidre Wilma York was startled to receive a visitor from the MacGregor estate, she had two alternatives either return all monies owed from her thievery or spend an indefinite stay in the MacGregor Dungeons.

Latin

SOME DAYS LATER AMELIA attended her second council meeting just in case there was something she could contribute. All the usual members were in attendance and the first order of business she noted was much more exciting than a cow or bull. It was a missive from King Macbeth however it was written in Latin. Hendry the abbot spoke fluent Latin and would normally translate however as he was away it fell to Leon Snipes to translate as he used to be a cleric.

Amelia sat beside Beiste and took a sideways glance at the parchment skimming the contents. Her eyes widened in surprise at the contents. The new king was very progressive.

Although Beiste knew she could read Gaelic and English, it had never occurred to her to mention she could also read Latin. She decided there was no need to tell him now as they already had Leon there to translate.

Beiste handed the missive to Leon, who looked over it thoughtfully and made a big show about it, so Amelia thought. She quietly waiting to hear his translation.

Leon stood, paused for a while then spoke: "It says by order of the King the MacGregors are to pay a small tithe to the church for pilgrimage to the holy land as is a divine mandate of Christian teachings and Celtic traditions. They must also set up an investment sum for the general upkeep of those in need within the shire. These monies are to be managed by the village council in each division." He paused and scrunched up his face, cleared his throat then continued. "There is also a discussion of the King affirming male inheritance laws of which he will discuss with chieftains once these laws are enacted."

Beiste looked at Leon and thanked him for his translation, then turned to discuss the missive content further with the council. Amelia was hoping Leon had other business to attend to so she could speak to the council, but she needed to urgently speak to Beiste privately.

"My dear chieftain, may I speak with you privately for a moment?" Amelia asked Beiste.

"Amie, Love, not now."

"But Husband, I must speak with you tis very urgent."

"Amie, we dinnae have time for this, there is much to ponder about this missive."

"Beiste, please, I need a private word with you." Her voice was more forceful.

"Amelia, Sweeting, if it is about a current matter, you have an equal say here so tell us now if not it can wait."

"Very well." Amelia looked about the room with all eyes on her and said in a loud voice, "What Leon just read out to you is *not* what is written on that missive. I would have told you privately, Beiste, to save any awkwardness but seeing as you're a stubborn oaf I will leave you with it!"

Leon's face went stark white, and the entire room went stone silent.

A look of confusion descended. Everyone looked from Amelia to Beiste and then to Leon, then they all scowled.

Leon spluttered, "Are you accusing me of lying?"

"I am and I suspect you've been lying to the MacGregors for some time with your false translations." Amelia swiftly stood and was already halfway to the door before Beiste could stop her. "And if I were you, Leon Snipes, I'd re-read that missive in its entirety before my husband separates your head from your body."

"This is outrageous, you, canna even read, you are a liar!" Leon's eyes shifted nervously.

Beiste slammed his fist on the table and said, "Be careful what you call my wife.'

Amelia had pulled the door open by this stage and turned back to address the room. "Actually Leon, I can read English, Gaels, and Latin better than you, it seems. If you will all excuse me, I have a very important herb garden to attend to." With that, she slammed the door shut and walked out muttering about useless council meetings.

The council room erupted into mayhem after she left.

"Dalziel please retrieve my wife so she can explain. I ken it willna be easy because she has worked herself up into a temper."

"Leon sit down and explain yourself." Brodie was already standing next to him holding his sword in hand and Leon started trembling.

The other men just looked dumbfounded, as if they did not know what to make of this meeting.

"The mistress kens three languages? Well, I'll be, she is smarter than the lot of us," Eoin Murray said.

"Aye clever and bonnie too," Marcus Baird added.

"But isn't that sacrilegious for a woman to ken Latin?" Gordon Buchanan asked.

"What'll you have me do? Make her unlearn her ability?" Beiste replied.

"But it undermines the rule of men if women ken more," Gordon said.

Beiste put an end to the discussion when he replied, "It also undermines the rule of men if some men," — he looked at Leon — "mean to deceive other men who canna read the language. I trust my wife has Clan interests at heart."

With that, the council sat silent.

By the time Amelia returned, Leon was ready to re-read the translation, and he did so in its entirety with Amelia listening in. The missive stated that tithe funds be set aside for religious pilgrimage and to support widows and orphans as is a Christian duty. These funds were to be managed by the chieftain and the abbot, not the village council as Leon had stated earlier. The King was also moving towards recognizing equal inheritance rights for women and all clans were to discuss the matter as it applied to their own clan members. Leon had left that out completely.

When asked why he lied, Leon stated he had not lied intentionally he had just paraphrased incorrectly. Amelia was not so trusting of his explanation, but the council seemed to accept it, so she let it go.

Beiste just gazed at his wife, totally enamored with her ability to surprise him.

Later in their bed, Beiste kissed her gently. "Tis proud beyond measure I am that you can read Latin. Your skill has already helped the clan. I finally have a translator I can trust," he said.

"What of Leon?" Amelia asked.

Beiste just shrugged. "For now, he will keep, he is related to the Buchanans and some village councilmen. They might get annoyed if you accuse any of their kin."

Beiste kissed Amelia again. "I hope you can teach me Latin someday."

"I would love to, Husband, when you have the time to learn a new tongue."

"Mayhap we can start now. I enjoy learning new things where your tongue is involved." A glint came to his eye. "Say something lusty to me in Latin. I want to observe how your tongue moves," Beiste said as he leaned over and slipped his tongue into her mouth.

Amelia slapped him and burst out laughing. "Get on with you, you randy beast!"

Beiste chuckled and pulled down the top of her chemise, exposing her breasts. He suckled the hard peaks until she was moaning and writhing beneath him. Then he flipped her onto her belly, pulled her hips up so she was on all fours. He knelt behind her, pushed his plaid to the side, sought her wet heat, and thrust to the hilt.

Amelia collapsed onto her elbows, moaning as they engaged in a rhythmic dance as old as time. Beiste leaned down to kiss his wife as she turned her head, seeking his lips. Soon they were engaged in a tangle of tongues that had nothing to do with learning Latin.

Chapter 19

Kin

Life back at the Keep settled into a peaceful lull. With the cooler weather, the clan was busy harvesting and hunting game for the winter months. Wallace Duncan's departure meant the Keep functioned efficiently, giving Amelia more time to dedicate to what she loved the most, her herbs and healing. She now split her days evenly between her healer's cottage and managing the domestic needs of running a Keep.

Amelia also recruited Sorcha to help her maintain records and accounts. She was finding Sorcha a quick study in her lessons. Sorcha's mind was sharp, absorbing everything with veracity. Beiste told Amelia in the past, he had hired tutors for Sorcha. They would stay for a sennight then report that she was slow and unteachable. Amelia knew the opposite to be true. Sorcha was not slow at all. It was the tutors who lacked the ability to educate.

It was a cool Autumn day, and Sorcha and Amelia were in the study. Amelia had just moved some books from a table when a letter fell out. She picked it up to put it back inside, then stilled. The broken wax seal of the missive bore the same symbolic markings of her brooch. She instantly opened the letter and had to sit down, for her knees trembled. The date of the letter suggested Beiste had the missive for at least a fortnight and never, not once, mentioned anything to her.

The content had the blood rushing from her face. *Her grandfather was coming to claim her.* Her heart soared with joy and then nervousness and then anger. *Why had Beiste kept this from her?* She knew they had been busy, but why would he not tell her something of this much importance? If they were coming, she would need to prepare the Keep, make sure they were received well, that she was dressed well. Suddenly, she was frantic and panicked. There was much to do.

Amelia had just gone in search of Beiste when the bells tolled, noting visitors were approaching. She and Sorcha went to the window and there, coming up the rise, were dozens of horsemen. They wore the same bright colors as her mother's *airisaidh*. Her eyes settled on the enormous man in the lead. He had overlong grey hair tied in braids and carried a battle axe behind him; three men flanked him, one she recognized immediately as Malise, the potter from the village. Although now he did not look like a potter, he wore the rich plaid and bore the bearings of a laird.

Sorcha tapped her arm, pointed to the men, then furrowed her brow in a question.

"Oh, Sister, they are my kin," Amelia whispered. Sorcha looked surprised.

"Come, we must make ourselves presentable. Let's go get Ma."

The Macleans

BEISTE, BRODIE AND Dalziel stood on the ramparts. They had received word two days prior from their scouts that the Maclean contingent was close to the Keep. Dalziel, ever the strategist, already had several men in place along the route, ensuring if the Macleans proved to be hostile, they would be turned away before they ever set foot at the Keep. Family or not, Beiste would not risk his wife being taken against her will. He did not give Amelia any warning, for he knew if he told her in advance, she would fret and then work herself into exhaustion. The Keep staff were prepared for this day. He wanted nothing to give her undue stress.

"I best go find my wife so she can meet her kin," Beiste said in a sombre voice.

When Beiste found Amelia, she looked radiant and beautifully dressed, with Orla's help. But when Amelia saw him, he braced, for she came storming over and berated him for his lack of sensitivity,

"How dare you not tell me my *seanathair* was coming? Why did you hide the letter from me? What if they dinnae like me?" she shouted, then punched him in the stomach, which only ended up hurting her hand. "Ouch." She winced. "Why are you so muscly? You, behemoth."

Her voice was rising, her face was turning red, then she burst into tears.

Beiste immediately pulled her to him. "Hush, Love, tis going to be all right, all will be well."

She sniffed. "I wish I had more time to prepare. Do you think they will like me?" Amelia raised her tear-filled eyes to him, genuinely asking the question.

Beiste replied, "If they dinnae like you, I will kill them all."

Amelia saw the look in her husband's eyes and realized he was serious. That just made her giggle.

Beiste took her face into his hands and whispered. "I will meet them first and when tis safe I will call you, all right?"

"Aye, Beiste, lead the way."

※

THE MAN WALKED IN THE *shadows once more, following the frenzied movement of bodies all around. The Keep was in a flurry of activity and once again he blended in, hidden in plain sight amidst the busyness. He made two observations. First, the new mistress had powerful kin, the Macleans in fact, and second, the Beiste was in love with his wife.*

He chuckled to himself. That would make what he was about to do even more enjoyable, for he would unleash the most amount of pain.

BEISTE WAITED FOR DALZIEL and Brodie to join him, then they walked out to the steps to greet the Macleans.

"Welcome. I am Beiste MacGregor. How can I help you?"

"Greetings chieftain MacGregor, I am *Gilleain na Tuaighe*, chieftain of the Macleans of *Mull*. These are my sons Gillebride, Bristi, and Malise. We seek an audience with me *ban-ogha* Amelia MacGregor. Her ma was my *nighean*, Iona. I ask that you let us see her."

Beiste acknowledged them and replied, "Tis my wife who will decide if she will see you or not."

Gilleain would normally be outraged, but he understood the MacGregor was making it known that in matters of kin he would defer to his wife. It was a rare move for a powerful chieftain to make, but a wise one. He stated his wife held equal footing here, and it was they who would need to meet with her approval if they wanted an audience.

Gilleain tried to hide his smile. He was pleased with the honor bestowed upon his granddaughter. Her husband was publicly acknowledging her authority as his wife and, by association, respected her as a Maclean. Gilleain knew then, Beiste MacGregor was a wise man.

He agreed. "Aye, we would like to meet your wife... *if* it pleases her." He gave an assessing look to Beiste.

"Amie, Sweeting." Beiste stretched out his arm as she walked out to meet him. Beiste reached around and pulled her close to him. "Amie, you determine what happens now. I will stand by your decision."

Amelia kissed his cheek. She then looked out at the four men and greeted them with a tentative smile and a wave.

Gilleain just stared at her for the longest time. It was as if he were staring at Iona. He tried hard not to cry. He watched the interaction between her and Beiste and knew she was in excellent hands.

Amelia stepped forward and stood strong and proud when she said, "Chieftain MacLean, tis wonderful to meet you. Please seek your rest and refreshment at our table. You are all welcome."

Gilleain could barely contain his excitement and in a gruff voice he boomed, "Och, call me Granda!"

Dalziel signaled to squires who moved forward to take the horses. Brodie signaled several men, and they ushered the Maclean retainers into the bailey. Beiste signaled to the cook, who hurried off to prepare the platters of food and ale.

Amelia instantly liked her kin, especially when they reached the top of the stairs and instead of shaking hands, Gilleain picked her up and gave her an enormous hug. He then physically carried her to her uncles, who each gave her hugs. When her feet finally touched the ground, she was giddy and grinning like a fool. Beiste instantly pulled her back to his side, practically snarling at the men.

Once inside the hall, festivities began.

As soon as Jonet saw the men, she smiled widely and greeted them. "Well, if it isn't the Macleans." She turned to Amelia and said, "That's who ye reminded me of that first day I saw you, Iona Maclean. She was one of my closest friends." The four men instantly recognized Jonet, for they had all met years earlier.

"Aye, my memory is slowly coming back to me. Iona looked exactly like you, with the same eyes. That day you arrived, I thought you were her."

"You kenned my Ma?" Amelia spoke reverently.

"Aye, we used to play together as children. Then when I married Colban we lost touch, but I met her again when Beiste was five. She even played with him a little. I never saw her after that."

Amelia sat between Beiste and her grandfather so she could talk to her kin better. They told tales of Iona when she was younger and tried to fill Amelia in on so much family history. Soon there was much merriment music and dancing and Amelia lapped it all up, every bit, knowing that she was finally reunited with her mother's kin.

More platters of hot food came out as everyone ate with gusto. There was pheasant and venison and a plethora of festive delicacies. After the meal, Malise apologized. He had to lie to her about who he was. He wanted to make sure she really was his niece.

"That day I saw you I wanted so much to ask if ye kenned my sister, but then that big brute of yours interfered." Malise motioned his head jovially toward Beiste, who just scowled in return. "Now, son, I am your uncle. I'll not have you scowling at your betters," Malise said. Which only made Beiste scowl more and all the men laughed.

"What happened to Iona?" Gilleain asked.

"She died during childbirth with my brother."

"Ye have a brother?" Gilleain's eyes lit with hope.

"I had a brother, but he died with her."

Gilleain's eyes dimmed as he mourned that bit of news.

Amelia stared off into the distance and said, "I wish Ma could be here today, *Seanathair*. Ma would be so happy to see you all. When she died, her last thought was of you and that I promise to find you all."

Gilleain became teary.

Amelia reached out, clasped his hand, and addressed her kin. "Ma always told me that when people are at death's door, they think only of those they love the most. In her last moments, she thought only of you."

The dais went quiet again, and tears could be seen shimmering in all their eyes.

Malise stood. "I propose a toast to my late sister, Iona Maclean."

Everyone toasted.

"And what of that cur Dunbar?" Gilleain asked.

"They were in love, but they promised him to another, tis tragic," Amelia replied.

"Tragic? He took advantage of my sweet daughter and made her his leman." Gilleain was getting worked up again.

Amelia touched his arm. "Twas a long time ago, *Seanathair*. Nothing can bring Ma back now. But I want to show you the box she gave me. These were her belongings, but I did not know who you all were."

They looked at Iona's things as if they were the pope's robes; it was that precious. Gilleain held the crest badge. "I gave this to Iona when she left for the abbey. It was to be worn at her wedding. Did you wear these on your wedding day?" he asked.

Amelia shook her head.

Gilleain gave Beiste a quelling look and Beiste frowned back.

Amelia explained, "Twas not his fault. I did not reveal the box to anyone when I came here."

Soon the music started playing, and the mood lightened. Amelia even talked her grandfather and uncles out of waging war with the Dunbars for making her mother a leman.

As the festivities continued, a course of special sweets and honey mead was served throughout the hall. There was much excitement over fare rarely served.

As people overindulged and over imbibed, they started making their way home. When the hall had emptied to only the family on the dais and a few retainers and serving staff, a special golden-colored dessert whiskey was served. It was a special blend of tangerine, cinnamon, honey, and almonds.

Amelia noticed a small cup of the golden drink had been placed in front of her. She looked around and saw that everyone on the dais had a similar cup, although none had consumed theirs. Beiste was busy talking to Fergus, her guardsman and Bristi, her uncle. Brodie and Orla were arguing over something, Jonet and Gilleain were talking amongst themselves, and Dalziel was talking to Gillebride and Sorcha.

Amelia was sitting with her uncle, Malise, who had been discussing a trading venture involving pots. She picked up the drink and noticed an odd smell, assuming it was from the spices she brought the cup close to her lips when Malise yelled, "Stop!" and swiped the cup out of her hand. It flew several feet away.

And that was when all hell broke loose.

It shocked Amelia. Everyone had turned to watch the commotion drawing their weapons and Amelia found herself instantly lifted out of her chair and placed behind Beiste, who was facing off with Malise.

"What the hell do you think you're doing?" Beiste roared.

"I was saving my niece's life," Malise yelled in reply.

Gilleain was on his feet and shouted, "What is the meaning of this?"

Bristi and Gillebride were at Gilleain's side, looking from Beiste to Malise. Amelia noticed Brodie had pulled Orla protectively to his side, and it was the first time the two of them were *not* arguing. Dalziel had Sorcha behind him. She was visibly shaken.

Malise said, "Someone just tried to poison your wife!"

Beiste paled.

Malise pointed at the cup. "Bitter almonds, I smelled it in her drink."

Beiste picked it up and smelled it too. Amelia had registered the faint scent, but they masked it with all the sweetened honey.

Beiste yelled orders, "Close off the Keep. I will question everyone who served tonight."

Dalziel and Fergus were already out the door to the kitchens.

Brodie checked all the other cups, sniffing them. "None of these smell the same as Amelia's."

Beiste gritted his teeth and pulled Amelia close. That meant she was the only target, her alone. This was the second time someone had tried to kill her. The first was on the road, the second now.

"Who would want to do such a heinous thing to my *ban-ogha*?" Gilleain asked, wanting to tear down half the Keep before finding the culprit. He looked at Beiste. "If you canna protect her, she is coming with us. If my son had not intervened, she would be dead."

Beiste shouted back, "No one is taking my wife anywhere."

"We'll see about that. I heard you practically forced her to wed you," Gilleain bellowed. Fear for Amelia's safety was too much for him to stay calm. He had just found the child of his beloved daughter and to almost lose her here was too much.

"Da, calm doon we get nowhere pointing fingers," Bristi said.

"Did you see who put the glass down near her?" Brodie asked Malise.

"No, we were busy talking and platters were coming and going. I just noticed that her drink smelled different from mine.

"How do we ken it wasn't one of your men?" Fergus piped in. He had returned from the kitchens with serving maids in tow and speculated, "Tis strange you appear now and then this happens?"

"What are you accusing us of? Trying to kill our own kin?" Malise was losing his temper.

Brodie gave Fergus a stern warning to keep his mouth shut, but Fergus carried on regardless.

"Mayhap there is a reason you wanted to reconnect so badly. Is she to inherit something?" Fergus asked.

"How dare your men accuse us of this? This happened in your Keep!" Gilleain shouted and pointed at Beiste.

Amelia could not get a word in, trying hard to see around Beiste. Now her uncles were also yelling and shouting in outrage.

"She's our kin. We would never harm her. If you canna protect her, then we will take her to *Mull*!" Malise yelled.

"I am her kin, and she is mine!" Beiste roared.

Everyone started shouting again. Then an unexpected thing happened.

Jonet stood on the table looking every inch a warrior of old and she swung high and brought down Gilleain's battled axe on the table, splintering the wood. The sound was enough to capture everyone's attention.

"Be quiet, all of you!" she yelled. "Tis enough to make me cast up my supper, what with all the bellowing."

"Ma!" Beiste came forward. "Get down from there."

"Give me that axe you, silly woman. You'll end up cutting yourself." Gilleain moved forward to take it, but Jonet raised it and swiped at him until he stepped away.

"Tis you men who need to quieten down. All of you sit down now!" she demanded.

They begrudgingly did. "And you, you boorish man, have not changed one bit, bellowing and carrying on, why you used to do the same to Amelia's *seanmhair* before she beat you with her broom, and then you ranted and raved at Iona like a dragon."

Stunned silence followed this. First, because Jonet was giving a set down to a room full of men and secondly because Jonet was lucid for a change.

"My Amelia has had a fright, and the people she loves are fighting each other instead of trying to find out who did this." Jonet pointed at Beiste and his men and said, "Start questioning those who had access to Amelia's drink and question the guards who were supposed to be watching the kitchens." Jonet then climbed down from the table. "Now, if someone will remind me where my blasted bedchamber is, I would be very grateful," she huffed.

Primal Need

SEVERAL HOURS AFTER Amelia's attack, they had interrogated everyone with no clear sign as to who could have poisoned Amelia's drink. Only the most trusted were allowed near Amelia and they increased security around the Keep. The Macleans were given guest chambers to stay in, and their retainers camped by the loch and formed another line of defense.

It was late in the evening after they had bathed. Amelia and Beiste were both still reeling from her attempted murder, and neither one of them would leave each other's side. The Keep had settled for the night and the aftermath had unleashed a primal need.

Beiste was lying on his back in their bed and Amelia was riding astride him. His hard, thick length was impaled deep inside her silken sheath. Her hands rested on his shoulders as her breasts bounced above his head as she rode him with abandon. Amelia's moans were coming in quick gasps as her hips moved faster.

"Aye, that's it, Love just like that." Beast encouraged, both hands gripping a rounded ass cheek, pulling her on and off his length to speed up the momentum. "You're so tight. You feel so good." He groaned as he slammed her down his length again and again. "That's it, Sweeting. I need you to come for me."

Amelia was lost in the euphoria. "Beiste, I need you to...."

"I've got you, Love." The sound of his voice was guttural. He braced his feet on the bed and thrust upwards, pounding her welcome heat as Amelia moaned louder.

Beiste growled, leaned his head forward, and laved her nipple with his tongue. He felt her body stiffen and contract so tight around him, he almost spilled.

Amelia was lost in a sea of ecstasy. Her husband's tongue against her breast sent shock waves of pleasure straight to her core. As Beiste's thrusts increased, the friction caused a powerful sensation in her womb and her body spasmed.

"Look at me *mo leannan*, look at me," he growled. She opened her eyes and met his gaze as he kissed her mouth, drowning her screams as she came.

Beiste felt Amelia's climax, which triggered his own. He thrust three more times before his body stiffened and he roared as his seed exploded, bathing her womb with his essence.

Amelia slumped across him, passed out with her head tucked under his chin. His heart was beating so hard he collapsed back against the bed, their bodies still connected, his arms around her, and he felt utterly sated.

Beiste had almost lost her this day, and the memory of it terrified him. If anything happened to Amelia, he knew he would not survive it. They were inextricably linked, heart, mind, body, and soul. Never in all his life had it ever been this good, not with any other, only Amelia, his wife, his lover, just his.

Beiste pulled the covers over their naked bodies, too exhausted to do anything else. He closed his eyes and whispered, "I love you, Amie, with all my heart." Then he fell asleep.

THE MAN IN THE CLOAK stood in the shadows, seething that his slave had failed again. She had not masked the poison well.

This time, she was standing naked in the middle of the cell. Both her wrists were bound by iron shackles. A long iron chain hung from a hook in the ceiling, pulling her arms above her head. She could not lean or sit or rest her limbs. She was completely at his mercy and control. Her back was bloodied from his vicious whipping. Usually, this was the moment he would dig his fingers into her hips and pound her from behind while her blood smeared his groin. But not tonight.

She moaned, she sobbed, she pleaded for the release only he could give. "Please, Master, I need you, please." Instead, he pushed her away from him.

"You failed. You have used up all your chances," he said. And with those parting words, he slit her throat.

The next morning, Deidre's battered body was found floating in the loch.

Chapter 20

Into the Darkness

For several days, the atmosphere in the Keep was stilted. Everyone was on high alert and extra precaution was taken to ensure the safety of those within the Keep. It had horrified the Keep staff to discover someone had slipped into their kitchens and tried to kill their mistress. Their protectiveness of Amelia increased. Beiste posted several guards in the kitchens, near water cisterns, and storerooms. Orla kept a strict eye on all the food prepared for the family and also took it upon herself to provide extra security for her friend. A skilled archer, she now kept her bow and quiver on her at all times and her dirk inside her boot. She began wearing trews and a tunic instead of dresses.

As far as Orla was concerned, Amelia was a sister to her. The one person other than Morag who had accepted her without reservation and that was a priceless treasure worth protecting.

The Macleans and the MacGregors seemed to get along well with no open hostility. Beiste found Gilleain and his sons to be wise and honest men, and they found the MacGregor chieftain to be reasonable. It was as if they were all cut from the same cloth. They all genuinely cared for Amelia, so guarding her was made easier.

Gilleain also savored the time with his granddaughter, often joining her at the healer's cottage for hours on end as they shared years of family history over-brewed tea and cake. Amelia's uncles had also taken to dropping in for visits and reminiscing about their sister, Iona, and their mother, Moira, over honey mead and sweet treats.

As the men gathered regularly in the council room, they went through the lists of suspects and motive for who would want Amelia dead and who would gain the most advantage if they murdered her. Could it be the Dunbars or someone from Iona's past? Could it be an enemy of the MacGregors? An enemy of the Macleans?

Unbeknownst to them all, it would not be a list that revealed the real perfidy within the Keep, but a single recollection of a past event.

Hope

A SENNIGHT AFTER THE attempted poisoning, Amelia awoke feeling nauseous. She leaped out of bed and ran to the basin, where she emptied the contents of her stomach. When she had finished, she rinsed her mouth and wiped it with a towel. She turned around to find Beiste standing perfectly still a few feet away from her and just staring.

"Are you well, Love?" He looked concerned.

"Aye, Husband, I have just been feeling sick in the mornings."

She walked towards him, and he wrapped his arms around her as she hugged him in return, resting her cheek on his chest, her arms around his waist.

"How long have you been feeling this way?"

"On and off for a while now, but usually tis just a queasy feeling that goes away, tis why I keep chewing mint and ginger."

"Sweetheart."

"Aye Husband."

"When was the last time you had your menses?"

Amelia froze, then looked up at him, trying to calculate in her mind. "Not since before I wed you," she whispered, still trying to come to terms with what the answer to his question meant.

How could she miss it? Nausea, sensitive breasts, and she was late for her menses, in fact, weeks late. When she looked at Beiste again, his eyes were sparkling with emotion. With a questioning glance, he held his breath.

Amelia's eyes instantly filled with tears as she nodded and smiled, giving him the confirmation he needed. The expression on her husband's face was something she wished she could capture for eternity. It was a look of reverence, elation, and love. *Pure love.*

Beiste wiped the tears from her eyes. "Sweeting, you carry my bairn." It was a statement, not a question.

"Aye, I do."

They stood in their bedchamber, wrapped around one another, filled with hope for the future.

THAT AFTERNOON, AFTER Beiste and Amelia shared their news with their family members, Amelia had gone to the solar to work on the books. Sorcha was helping her. Orla was sitting by the fireplace binding flint arrowheads to notches in the arrow staff.

Jonet was sipping a saffron tea blend Amelia had mixed for her to improve her memory. Beiste and Gilleain had also come in to check on Amelia, for the fourth time, and decided to just stay put.

Amelia was trying to focus on figures when Jonet said, "Colban, my husband used to do that."

"Do what?"

"He would frown just like you are doing now whenever he went over the books."

"What was Colban like?" Amelia asked.

"He was just like Beiste." Jonet motioned to her son, slouched in a chair by the corner. "Always scowling or bellowing."

Amelia smiled at that comment she could just imagine.

"Where is Colban?" Jonet asked wistfully.

"He passed away, Jonet, but I ken he is still very much missed."

"Och aye, my poor Colban. They killed him, you ken. Almost home, then set upon by mercenaries."

"Aye, I heard, tis very sorry I am for your loss, Jonet."

There was a pause, and then Jonet said, "Sorcha was beside herself. Poor child, she had a huge fright when her da died."

Amelia sensed Sorcha stiffen beside her, and her breathing became shallow, almost panicked.

"You never spoke again. Did you, Love?" Jonet looked at Sorcha, who shook her head in response. "Colban's brother, Ludan, tried to save him, but it was no use. He was already dead."

Beiste joined the conversation and corrected her. "Ma, Uncle Ludan was not with Da. We never found the mercenaries."

"No, Son. Twas Ludan, who told me the news. I saw him come out of one of the private chambers that day and he told me Colban was dead."

Beiste looked at Jonet with a questioning frown. "Ma, mayhap you are confused. Uncle Ludan was in Northumbria when Da died."

"I am not confused, Son! I ken what I saw. Ludan was here, and he told me the news... didn't he?"

Sensing Jonet's distress, Gilleain intervened. "Son, if your ma says she saw him, then she saw him."

Jonet settled again and went back to sipping her tea and staring out the window.

Provoking the Bear

A DAY LATER, BEISTE was holding a private meeting with Dalziel, Brodie, and Shaun Douglas, who represented the guards. They were going over petitions from retainers.

Shaun said, "I have a petition here from Ranalf, tis about property."

Brodie looked bored. They had just gone through a dozen matters.

Beiste asked, "What does he request?"

"He requests a cottage closer to the woods."

"Why?" Dalziel asked.

"He is looking to secure himself a wife and would prefer they lived closer to the woods," Shaun replied.

Brodie wore a disinterested expression.

Beiste asked, "Who is the lucky lady?"

"Orla," Shaun replied.

"No," Brodie instantly interjected. The room went quiet as all eyes moved to Brodie.

Beiste raised an eyebrow. "Do you object to the house or the woman?"

Brodie replied, "Both. Ranalf has too many duties to see to right now. He should not be thinking of home and hearth."

Shaun interrupted, "But that should not stop him from marrying. He canna stay single forever."

"I said no!" Brodie stated emphatically, leaving no further room for discussion.

Dalziel and Beiste glanced at one another, not sure what was going on with their brother.

"Tis not like you to be mean-spirited, Brodie," Dalziel replied.

Brodie clenched his jaw and replied, "As Head Guardsman, I get the final say, and I have said it. Move on now, Shaun."

The men just shrugged and continued down the list. When they adjourned for a meal break, Brodie stood and left the room. He had something to do, and it could not wait.

On Target

ORLA WAS DOWN BY THE archery range again, testing the new arrows she had made. It was not long before she felt the familiar presence of her nemesis. *Why must he always interrupt her quiet times?*

Brodie knew he would find Orla here. He walked up to her, and even before she could turn around, he demanded answers. "I heard you are looking to wed?"

"What's it to you what I plan to do?"

"Tis true, then you're in love with Ranalf?"

She turned towards him. "Brodie Fletcher, I dinnae ken how that is any of your concern."

"Anything to do with my guardsmen is my concern, Orla." He was moving closer, and she was standing her ground.

Orla did not know what was going through his head. She did not even know what she felt about Ranalf, but it was none of Brodie's affair. "Ranalf and I are just courting, he's a kind man, he has shown interest." She shrugged her shoulders.

"Have you been sleeping together?" Brodie's jaw ticked with the thought of Ranalf touching Orla, at the thought of *any* man touching her.

Orla stopped and glared at him as if he had two heads. "That has nothing to do with you. I prefer this conversation ended now." She was stomping down the target range to pick up her arrows as he followed beside her.

"Keep your hands off my men, Orla! They canna be distracted by the likes of you," he snapped.

Orla whipped her head around. "What do you mean by the likes of me?" She gritted her teeth. "Am I not good enough for your men, Brodie?"

Brodie stumbled slightly. "No, I didna mean it like that... I just meant you ken being —"

"Being what, Brodie? Spit it out." Orla was getting mad, beyond annoyed, ready-to-stab-him-in-the-eye-with-an-arrow, mad.

Orla stared off with the Bear, daring him to say whatever offensive, invective thing he was about to say.

Brodie was silent, utterly lost for words because he could not give her one reasonable explanation why he wanted her to stay away from his men, from *all* men. He paused too long and realized too late, because Orla had come to her own conclusion by then.

"I understand perfectly. Your men are too good for a mixed-raced Viking bastard like me. That's what you meant to say!" Orla picked up her bow and arrows and turned to him once more. "You can go to hell, Brodie Fletcher, because none of you will *ever* be good enough for me!" With those parting words, Orla turned on her heels and ran back to the Keep.

"Damn it!" Brodie cursed. *Why did their interactions always have to turn to shit?*

⁂

Pieces

WHEN THE MEN RETURNED to complete the petitions list, Beiste still had questions about what Jonet told him the previous day.

"Shaun, the morning of my da's death, who was guarding the Keep?"

"Twas Gil and his men, but there had been a mishap on the road. A cart turned over, blocking the entrance to the burn. Twas the only time they left their post."

"And who was with my da when he died?"

"Fergus, Drew and Shamus."

"Why did he not have his full guard?" Beiste asked.

Shaun replied, "Halfway home, word came that the Keep was under attack. Your da was already injured from an earlier skirmish and could not ride fast, so he sent us ahead. Fergus agreed to stay with Drew and Shamus to guard your da. We were so close to home, they deemed it safe to split up."

"So, what happened?" Brodie asked.

"They were set upon straight after we left. Drew and Shamus were killed only Fergus survived, but they hit him on the head, and he could not recall much."

Something did not sound right. Beiste asked, "What happened when you reached the Keep?"

"When we arrived, the Keep was fine, twas no attack."

Beiste thanked Shaun and excused him from the room.

As soon as the door shut behind him, Dalziel said, "Twas a diversion. To separate your da's guards."

Brodie agreed. "Aye, it left your da vulnerable and readily able to be taken by mercenaries."

Beiste said, "What if there were no mercenaries at all?"

"What are ye suggesting?" Dalziel asked.

Beiste replied, "We found no sign of them, which is strange, but now Ma is remembering things thanks to Amelia's care. She swears Ludan, my uncle, was here that morning in the Keep. He told her Da was dead."

"Why is that strange to you?" Dalziel asked.

"Ludan told everyone he was going trading in Northumbria that day."

"Are you thinking mayhap Ludan had something to do with your da's death?" Brodie asked.

"Tis a possibility," Beiste replied.

Dalziel said, "But what would he gain from killing your da? He still would inherit nothing because you are the heir."

The three men pondered his last thought.

"Ludan was also here the night Caitrin died," Beiste said. "The circumstances of her death still seem strange to me now. She had guards with her all the time. She was overjoyed about the bairn. Why would she abort?"

Dalziel remarked, "If Ludan wanted to inherit the title, he would need to get rid of Colban, and you, and any of your heirs. So far, your da, your late wife and your unborn bairn have all passed. Why not just get rid of you now?"

Brodie replied, "Because he has guards and us around him all the time." Brodie sat up straight. "Brothers, there's something else that's even more concerning."

"What's that?" Beiste and Dalziel asked in unison.

"According to Shaun, Fergus was one of your da's guards on the day he died. He was the only one to survive the attack. Fergus was also guarding Caitrin on the night she died, twas supposed to be Kieran, but he came down sick with a stomach ailment."

Beiste could already feel his heart thundering in his chest when he said, "Fergus was also present on the attack on Amelia outside of Glasgow and he was the last person to check on the prisoner he claims ran away."

Dalziel replied, "He was also guarding Amelia the night her cup was poisoned."

"Fuck!" Beiste cursed. "Where is Fergus right now?"

Brodie's face paled. "He's watching Amelia this afternoon. She was heading to the village with Sorcha and Orla."

"Who else is with them?" Beiste demanded.

"Lachlan and Ranalf are also on duty. They should at least be able to protect her," Brodie replied as the three of them bolted for the door.

As they were running down the stairs, they entered the Great Hall and saw Lachlan of all people standing near a table where Jonet sat.

Beiste roared, "Why the bloody hell are you not guarding Amelia?"

Lachlan looked confused. "I was not assigned, Amelia. I am to watch Jonet today?"

"Who told you that?" Brodie yelled.

"Fergus, he... he said plans had changed, and I was to stay here. He went with Ranalf. Why what's happened?"

With no time to explain, Beiste, Brodie and Dalziel headed straight for the stables.

Perfidy

AMELIA HAD BEEN FEELING under the weather again that morning, so she decided to just spend a few hours in the solar instead of going to the healer's cottage, which had been the original plan. Her grandfather and uncles were down by the loch, seeing to their retainers. Orla and Sorcha would go with her later to the village, and Beiste and his men were busy in meetings. She sent a message earlier with Ranalf to let the others know where she was and the change in plans.

Amelia was just making notes when a shadow crossed over her. She turned in fright. "Oh, it's just you. You scared the life out of me, Fergus."

"Sorry Mistress, but tis time to head to the village," Fergus said.

"Oh aye, I'll just go to my room and freshen up quickly." Amelia walked to her chambers, noting that something seemed off about Fergus. He was not his jovial self, but then maybe he had a lot on his mind. She got ready and donned the MacGregor *airisaidh* pinned together with her Maclean brooch.

When Amelia opened the chamber door, she looked around and did not see anyone else. She walked down the hallway and called out, "Fergus? Are you there?"

"Here, Mistress, I just had to check a few things."

"Where are the others?" Amelia asked.

"Lady Sorcha and Orla said they will meet us at the stables."

Amelia nodded, not thinking much of it. As she walked down the hallway, she swore she heard Morag's voice. She whipped her head back but saw no one. Then she heard Morag's voice again. This time it was like a whisper in her ear saying, "Guard your bairn, Amelia, he wants your bairn." Then the voice disappeared.

She looked at Fergus. "Did you hear that?" she asked.

Fergus just shrugged that he did not know what she was talking about.

Amelia shook her head in confusion, thinking she must be hearing things. She kept walking, then paused. *Her bairn? Who wanted to harm her bairn?* She looked up at Fergus and saw a strange look in his eye she had never seen before. Amelia suddenly felt frightened and turned to run when a blinding pain exploded in the back of her head. Then everything went black.

SORCHA HAD WAITED PATIENTLY in her chambers for a guard to take her to the healer's cottage. That is where they had all planned to meet before going to the village, but no one appeared. She glanced out her door to see the hallway was empty. She grabbed her things and stepped outside. Sorcha could see no one and really did not want to miss a trip to the village, so she headed off by herself.

She was just coming down the back stairwell when she saw Amelia slumped over someone's shoulder and they were entering one of the unused chambers on the top floor. The hairs on the back of her neck stood on end. Something was not right.

Sorcha quietly followed, then peeked inside. But there was no one there. She crept into the room and looked around, but it was empty. Then she heard it, the sound of voices laughing and talking behind the wall. They were going to hurt Amelia. She needed to get help fast.

Sorcha ran without thinking. She needed to find Beiste. She was flying down the stairs when she ran straight into Orla. Sorcha gestured wildly.

"Sorcha, slow down. What's the matter?" Orla asked.

Sorcha grabbed Orla by the hand and pulled her towards the chamber. She motioned to the wall. She mouthed the name Amelia and with frantic hand gestures pointed to her ear.

Orla could hear the voices too, but they were very faint, moving further away.

"Amelia? You saw someone carry her behind this wall?" Orla asked.

Sorcha nodded.

Orla started looking around the wall for a way to open it. Frantically pressing everything to see if she could find an entryway when she stumbled over something sticking out of the skirting board. When Orla looked down, she saw a small latch. She pulled it and heard a click. When she pushed on the stone wall, it slowly moved inwards, allowing an opening big enough for a person to fit through.

They both looked on astonished.

Orla turned to Sorcha and said, "Go get help. Find Beiste or any of the others and do it quickly."

Sorcha nodded and took off running as Orla plunged headfirst into the darkness.

WHEN AMELIA REGAINED consciousness, she knew she was in trouble. Her mind was still foggy, and she winced from the pain in the back of her head, but she was otherwise all right. She was sitting on a hard-stone floor propped up against a stone wall. She instantly reached for her tummy and noted nothing was amiss. Her bairn was all right. She needed to keep things that way. Amelia surveyed her surroundings. She was in a large, dimly lit room with wide-open doors. She could just make out a passageway beyond the doors. A small candle flickered in the darkness. She had an iron shackle around her wrists attached to a chain on the wall and there were weapons or some tools near the far wall. It was cold and dank, and she smelled the metallic scent of blood.

Some time passed when a figure emerged from the dark.

"Fergus? Why are you doing this?" she asked.

"Mistress, you are bonnie when you're curious, tis what the master wants."

"Who is your master?"

"He's the one you need to worry about."

Amelia shuddered. This man was a maniac. "What does he want with me?"

"He hired us to make sure you dinnae get the chance to birth any bairns. But the way you two have been rutting tis a good possibility we are too late."

Amelia stiffened. "Who's we?"

"Why tis me and my brother," Fergus replied, just as a cloaked man emerged from the shadows. The same person Amelia saw the first day she arrived at the Keep. Amelia trembled when he drew back his hood.

"Surprise!" Ranalf howled with glee.

The person standing before her was not the placid Ranalf she knew. This one was cold and assessing. There was nothing in his eyes but violence. He scared Amelia right down to her marrow.

ORLA STUMBLED INTO the darkness, feeling like the walls were closing in on her. She fought hard not to panic. She hated the dark, but for now; it concealed her. Orla did not know where she was going, she just kept moving downwards. It was necessary for her to get to Amelia. She held her dirk in her hand as she felt her way along the walls. She saw a light up ahead and she could hear murmuring voices. Then she heard a piercing scream. All fear of the darkness left as Orla stumbled faster towards the light.

RANALF SLAPPED AMELIA across the face hard, then held her chin with a crushing grip. His dead eyes stared directly at hers. "Scream for help again, bitch, and I'll gut you right here."

Amelia instinctively looked contrite. Ranalf pushed her away from him and ordered his brother to stand her up. Fergus did his bidding.

Amelia now stood hooked to the ceiling with iron manacles around her wrists and no matter how she tried to wriggle, she could not ease the restraints. They stretched her arms above her head, and she stood almost on tiptoes, trying to remain standing to ease the pain in her shoulders. Ranalf left the room to get his whip. He wanted Amelia compliant when he whipped the bairn out of her.

Unlocking

SORCHA REACHED THE Great Hall. It was mostly empty.

Jonet called to her, "Sorcha stay here, Amelia is missing, Beiste and the others are headed to the cottage—"

Before Jonet could finish, Sorcha was already running out of the Keep. It was there she spotted Beiste and his men in the distance down by the stables. She knew they headed to the wrong place. She tried to yell, but nothing came out.

The quickest way to Beiste was to run straight through the training grounds and not around the safety barrier, so she did just that. Sorcha ran straight into the midst of all the trainees' sparring and weapons clashing. She dodged and weaved her way, eyes on her brother and his men. Sorcha waved her arm in desperate gestures; she heard yelling as men amid sparring almost cut her. Some stopped while others, oblivious to her presence, continued; she ran on.

Sorcha heard the melee of clashing swords, iron against iron, and steel against steel. The thundering sounds of combat and metal pierced a memory hidden so deep it dislodged itself from within the recesses of her mind. It transported Sorcha back to that day they killed her father.

Vivid images from years past assaulted her all at once. Images she had fought so hard to banish from her mind refused to remain hidden. She remembered now. She had snuck out of the Keep and was hiding in the bushes by the side of the road, waiting to surprise him. Her father was coming home.

Sorcha remembered swords clashing against shields and blood, so much blood. Fergus fought two guards while her uncle, Ludan, bludgeoned her father with an axe to the back of the head. She watched as her father staggered and fell to his knees on the side of the road. She witnessed the horrified expression in his eyes when he stared right at her. Fear for her safety etched his features. His right hand reached up to his mouth, an index finger pressed against his lips, and he uttered his last word to her before he died, "Shh."

Sorcha remembered staying hidden for hours, willing herself not to move, not to scream, not to speak.

As her memory unlocked, so did her voice. A release of all the fear and the rage and the terror. Her silence served a purpose then, but only her voice could help Amelia now.

Sorcha came back to the present. She saw Beiste about to mount his destrier. She took a deep breath, parted her lips, and let the air expel from her lungs to rattle life back into disused vocal cords. And she screamed, "Beiste!... Beiste!... Beiste!"

Everyone stilled at the sound of the scream, which was louder than any battle cry.

Beiste was stunned to hear Sorcha speak, let alone shout, but he ran towards her and picked her up. "I'm here, tell me."

"Someone took Amelia, a secret door. Orla has gone too. Help them!"

Beiste placed Sorcha on the ground, and together they sprinted for the Keep.

"Bloody hell!" Brodie cursed and followed close behind.

Pitch Black

ORLA ENTERED A SERIES of cells following the light and the sound of voices. She crept into the darkness, needing to get a closer look inside the room where she knew Amelia must be. She was mindful not to be seen. As she got closer, she could make out the figure inside. It was Fergus. *What the hell was he doing?* She put her dirk back into her boot and quietly pulled her bow and arrow from her quiver instead. She could take down one man easily.

Orla stood just outside the wide doorway and had a clear shot of Fergus, who was walking around the cell. She aimed and fired, but the mark went wide because the stinging pain of a whip cut across her bow arm as her bow clattered to the ground.

Ranalf stepped out of the shadows as he pushed her against the wall, his hand tightly gripping her neck. Orla tried to kick him, but he subdued her. She tried to get him to release her neck, but his hand would not budge; he seemed to become more excited the more she fought him, and he squeezed harder.

"Well, look what we have here? My, what providence is this?" He released her neck, and she gulped in air and started coughing, then he pushed her against the wall again. This time, he was inches from her face, caging her with his entire body. "How I've always wanted to see bloody red stripes on darker skin. I have longed to play with you."

Orla could feel something hard poking her stomach. He was becoming aroused. *What kind of sick game was this?* "You need to let us go, Ranalf. Beiste and his men will be here soon."

Ranalf laughed before he placed the palm of his hand across her neck and his mouth came crashing down on hers. He bit her lip until it bled. She winced and pulled her head away. He just licked the blood. "When I'm done with her, I will take my time with you," he said.

Orla shuddered. This was not the man who courted her with gentle words. She moved into a better position and kneed him in the groin. Ranalf shouted in pain and doubled over; she tried to move away, but he grabbed her hair and rammed her head against the wall.

Orla collided with the stone so hard she almost passed out. Ranalf took advantage of her dazed state. He grabbed his whip, and began whipping her in a frenzied attack. Orla fell to the ground, curling into a ball, trying to stay conscious and trying to protect herself from the stinging cuts.

Amelia screamed, "Stop it! Stop it!"

Ranalf seemed to come back to his senses. He stopped and was panting. He kicked Orla hard in the ribs twice.

Orla heard something crack, and she passed out from the pain.

BEISTE AND BRODIE DESCENDED the stairs as Dalziel waited with Sorcha, guarding the entryway. Dalziel had orders to kill anyone who came out that was not them. With the discovery of the passageway, none of them knew what to expect or even who could work against them.

Both men let their eyes adjust to the darkness, then started moving fast. The passage wound around the inner burn of the building. Beiste could not believe he only learned of this now. Whoever used it could slip in and out of the Keep and between rooms undetected.

When they came to the lighted area, they slowed and stayed quiet, listening before they entered. It was then Beiste heard it, the whipping sound and Amelia shouting for someone to stop. Both of them were already through the door.

Brodie roared when he realized it was Orla lying unconscious on the ground. He ran towards Ranalf and knocked him out with the back of his axe. He raised it again to finish him off when Fergus roared, "Stop or I kill her now!"

Beiste and Brodie paused when they saw Fergus holding Amelia's hair back with one hand and holding a dagger across her neck with the other.

Beiste could not, would not, risk Amelia's life or their bairn. He needed to stay calm and think.

"Now you will throw your axe over here," Fergus said to Brodie.

Beiste signaled Brodie to do it. Brodie glared at Beiste in refusal, giving a silent warning, but Beiste shook his head and said, "Do it now, Brodie."

Brodie reluctantly threw the axe near Fergus's feet.

"And you will shackle yourself to that wall," Fergus instructed.

Brodie looked irritated but did as requested.

"And you, Chieftain, will drop your sword and step into the light."

Beiste did so.

Ranalf slowly came to. He stood on shaky feet but made his way inside the room where Fergus held Amelia and where Beiste now stood.

Chapter 21

Out of the Darkness

Fergus laughed, and it sounded more like a cackle. "That's right, you prick. I'll gut your pregnant wife like I did your last."

"What do ye mean?" Beiste asked.

"Master wanted the babe gone. Deidre just had to slip a few drops of pennyroyal into Caitrin's tea that night. But the bitch still would not die, so I cut her to make sure she did."

Beiste felt sick to his stomach over what he was hearing. The man was a murderer and had no remorse. Caitrin and his babe were murdered, and it was Beiste who left her in the hands of a madman.

"You will die this day where you stand," Beiste stated calmly.

Fergus burst out laughing. "You think you can kill me? With what? Look around you." He spat. "We have all the power now." Fergus pulled Amelia's hair harder. She winced, and Beiste wanted to kill him even more.

Amelia was so relieved to see Beiste. His presence in that room was calming, and she knew her husband would rescue her. She had faith in his abilities. She knew to remain quiet and not do anything that could interfere with whatever he had planned.

"Do you have any last words to say?" Beiste asked Fergus.

Fergus stared at Beiste as if he were mad. "I dinnae need last words tis you who needs them, Chieftain."

Beiste heard a movement behind him and knew it was Ranalf. No doubt the man had regained his senses after the hit to the head, but he also knew Ranalf was still a little groggy. Ranalf shuffled as if unsteady, and Beiste knew it was why he had not attacked from behind... yet. Beiste needed to work fast. He could not afford to have Ranalf at full capacity.

"So, who is your master? Is it Ranalf over here?" Beiste gestured to his right side where Ranalf stood. It gave him time to see what weapons Ranalf possessed. The whip was gone, but a sword still hung by a scabbard.

Ranalf chortled. "Our master is your uncle Ludan and once you and your wife are dead, he will be the new chieftain here."

Beiste spoke in a deadpan voice, "That will not happen, because I will kill you both for murdering my late wife and my unborn bairn and I will kill you Fergus for hurting the woman I love."

Amelia looked up at Beiste with unshed tears and complete trust shimmering in her eyes.

"You and whose war band?" Fergus guffawed.

"I dinnae need a war band, Fergus."

"Ha, then how do you suppose you'll achieve that?" Fergus scoffed.

Beiste replied, "Easy, you will die by your brother's sword but before you do, you will live long enough to watch him felled by that axe." Beiste nodded towards the axe on the floor next to Fergus's feet.

Beiste then looked at Amelia and calmly said, "Close your eyes, Love."

Amelia stared at him a second, seeing the deathly serious look on his face, and did as he asked.

Both brothers burst out laughing.

As the seconds ticked by, Beiste did not react at all. He just patiently waited for the opening, which he knew would come. He had trained for war his entire life and never had a battle been more important than this one.

Beiste slowed down his breathing and focused on all the steps in his mind. Every minute detail of the room he committed to memory. He heard only the beating of his heart and the rhythmic breathing of each man. He focused all his energy from his mind to his hands through his body.

Fergus stopped laughing and, in a blink of an eye, he moved the dagger away from Amelia's neck and raised it in the air, ready to stab the blade into her stomach. It was then Fergus knew he had made a mistake.

In a split second, Beiste turned and unsheathed Ranalf's sword from its scabbard at the same time Beiste's other hand punched Ranalf in the side of his head. Ranalf hit the floor and was struggling to get back up when Beiste ran towards Fergus and swung the sword, severing Fergus's raised arm.

Fergus staggered back and yelled in pain as the blood spurted from the open wound. He stared in shock at his severed limb lying on the floor, his hand still clasping his dagger.

Without hesitation, Beiste twirled the sword around and plunged it into Fergus's chest. He then shoved his foot under the axe lying near Fergus's feet, kicked it up into the air, and grabbed the handle with both hands. He turned and braced to battle Ranalf, who was coming at him with a dirk.

Fergus was still standing, staring in disbelief at his brother's sword now embedded in his chest. He looked up just in time to watch Beiste sever Ranalf's head from his body with the axe. As his brother's head rolled across the ground, Fergus cried in anguish, making a gurgling sound as blood began dripping from his mouth. He collapsed onto the floor, dead.

Beiste dropped the axe and moved towards Amelia; her body was shaking uncontrollably. She was whimpering, but her eyes remained firmly closed. He was glad that, for once, his woman did as she was told.

"Amie, Love, 'tis all right. You are safe now," he said. "Keep your eyes closed."

Beiste immediately removed the shackles, and she dropped her arms in relief, then cried. He lifted her into his arms.

"Ca... ca... can I open my eyes now?" she asked, sniffing and hiccupping.

"No Love, not yet, I'll tell you when." He carried her out of the room and released Brodie before he let her open her eyes.

Brodie did not hesitate. He gently picked up Orla, held her close against his chest, and carried her out of the darkness.

Beiste did the same with his wife.

A MONTH HAD PASSED since the horrific incident of that day. The hidden passageways were now sealed. Orla had recovered from her injuries and was away spending time with Morag. As the first winter frost had arrived, the Macleans and their retainers took their leave with great affection on both sides and promises of future visits to the *Isle of Mull*. Amelia was slowly increasing, and the promise of tiny feet brought excitement to the Keep.

Beiste was subdued. The elation of becoming a father could not stamp out the trepidation of someone harming his wife and unborn bairn. If his protectiveness was stifling before, it was suffocating now. Many an argument could be heard between the chieftain and his wife over the number of restrictions placed upon her movements.

Sorcha had finally spoken of her ordeal to her family. Everyone had remained quiet as she recounted the horror of her father's death.

The council met several times to discuss ways of bringing Ludan to justice for his crimes. It was a complicated issue, as charges laid against a nobleman needed careful consideration. However, the decision was taken out of their hands because not long afterward a missive arrived from the 'Red King' Macbeth, and within it a summons to Court for Amelia MacGregor. Her accuser was none other than Ludan MacGregor and the charges laid against her was that of witchcraft.

Chapter 22

Macbeth's Castle – Dunsinane, Perthshire - *Two weeks later*

Into the Light

Amelia shuddered at the sight of the ominous castle on top of Dunsinane Hill. An impenetrable monolithic fortress, it terrified her to think of the dangers within its walls.

Beiste felt her stiffen and wrapped his arm around her tighter. "Courage Amie, I'll not be far *mo cridhe*." She had traveled most of the journey sitting with him atop *Lucifer* and she had never felt safer. Amelia only hoped she could return with her husband when this was over.

The following morning, having been summoned by the King, Amelia stood in the center of the Great Hall while Beiste sat with the other courtiers. She had never seen such finery. From the lavers at the entranceway to the rose petals strewn across the floor. Gold-painted walls displayed resplendent colorful tapestries and banners. The high table on the dais was intricately carved and adorned with silverware. The furniture about the room was brightly colored with materials that could only have come from far-off lands.

The royal thrones were carved with immaculate heraldic designs. Although lavish in its decor the castle interior retained an understated opulence. The owners exercised restraint, so the grandeur was not garish but refined. Servants and stewards lined the walls, ever ready to meet the whims of Royal Court.

Amelia watched as King Macbeth entered the room. Everyone stood. Macbeth walked straight to his Queen Gruoch *ingen* Boite. He kissed her cheek and silent words passed between them. There was no mistaking the genuine affection he held for his wife. He then took his seat beside her.

Amelia finally came face to face with the Scottish king. They called him 'The Red King' for his fighting ability to turn battlefields blood red. She had to admit he was a handsome man, fair-haired and tall with a ruddy complexion. His eyes were assessing, but they were not unkind.

Amelia curtsied low and greeted him with, "Your Majesty."

"Please sit, all of you sit." Macbeth signaled to a page and a seat was brought forward. Amelia sat and so did everyone in the hall.

"Now then there is no need to stand on ceremony, call me cousin for we are kin are we not?" he said.

"Aye, Cousin," Amelia replied.

"And permit me to be frank, but you are Maldred's illegitimate daughter?"

"Aye, your Maj... I mean, Cousin."

"I have heard they miss you in Dunbar, your healing skills are reputed to be remarkable. Your *màthair* was raised in an Abbey I presume for her healing ways were exceptional."

It surprised Amelia that Macbeth knew about her mother. "How did you ken?" she asked.

"I have my sources, but I was also raised in a Christian monastery from the age of seven and taught by monks. I ken when talented healers have been taught by an exceptional religious order."

Amelia was not sure where this line of conversation was heading, but she remained calm.

"Did your *màthair* pass anything onto you from the Abbey?" the King asked. "My sources tell me it was Iona Abbey in the *Isle of Mull*."

"Aye, she did. Twas a book of healing methods and remedies, written in Latin and it formed the basis of a lot of her healing knowledge."

Amelia glanced at the dais and caught the Queen watching her intently. She did not know whether to smile or look down, but then the Queen gave her a quick wink then her face became serious again. Amelia was not sure if she imagined it, but it lifted her spirits somewhat. She smiled tentatively then looked back at Macbeth who seemed very relaxed sitting back on his throne as if this were a minor matter he needed to complete.

Eventually Macbeth with a booming voice addressed the Court. "Amelia MacGregor, you have been called before this Royal Court to answer serious charges laid by a nobleman, that of witchcraft. If found guilty, the penalty is death or imprisonment. Both outcomes would mean they would strip your husband of his lands and chieftainship for consorting with a known witch."

The crowd began murmuring. Amelia paled and looked at Beiste and he just looked angry.

"How do you plead to these charges?" Macbeth asked.

Amelia stood. "I am not guilty Your Majesty, I have never used witchcraft on anyone. All my knowledge I attained from my *màthair*, and she was no witch." She sat back down.

"There must still be a formal hearing. All you need to refute these claims is someone to speak in your favor that your healing methods are not mere magic or sorcery. It must be someone who has seen your practice first-hand and kens them to be genuine," Macbeth said.

Amelia looked at Beiste. He just gave her an encouraging smile. They had witnesses with them, but she was not sure it would be enough.

"Right then, shall we get started?" Macbeth stood and ushered people to the dais. There was a Commissary who would preside over proceedings. The crowd whispered as he approached the dais. With him was a tall thin reedy man Amelia had never seen before. He had inky hair and cold eyes. She shivered when he walked past her and sneered. He could only be her accuser.

The presiding Commissary read out the charges of witchcraft and then called forth Ludan MacGregor to state his claim.

Ludan stood before the Court smugly garbed in his finery consisting of a long colorful plaid. "This woman put a spell on my nephew and his entire family. Overnight my nephew has turned from a battle-hardened warrior to a simpering lovesick sop," Ludan said.

Beiste growled and glared at his uncle.

Ludan continued. "He is unfit to rule. I request that I be installed as chieftain of the MacGregors because of my relationship to my late brother, Colban MacGregor, who would be appalled by my nephew's behavior."

"You lying sack of shite," Beiste yelled and had to be restrained by guards.

"What proof do you have that she is a witch?" King Macbeth asked.

"I call upon witnesses who have seen her evil sorcery first-hand."

Amelia watched as a woman approached, her head was covered in a veil, and when she lifted it, it was Elora.

Elora testified saying, "I have seen Amelia MacGregor work her magic over the chieftain. Before he met her, it was I who warmed his bed every night several times a night, and he promised I would rule by his side but after meeting her he began chanting her name and lighting candles at night with a vacant expression upon his face."

"You speak with a forked tongue, what has my uncle paid you?" Beiste shouted before the guards silenced him. Beiste cursed. This was a farce.

"Brother, remain calm." Dalziel appeared at his side. "We will not let them harm her over lies."

"Have you any other witnesses?" the Commissary asked Ludan.

"I call a Mr. Wallace Duncan."

Wallace stepped forward and similar to Elora he gave false testimony. "I was a trusted advisor and estate manager until that witch cast a spell over the chieftain. He stopped accepting my advice and listened to her, a woman. Tis sacrilegious that she can read Latin the holy language, only magic could have taught her such things. Tis evil to allow women education for it places them above men and God doesna allow it."

King Macbeth interrupted, "Then what say you of Latin speaking nuns? They are educated women in service to God."

Wallace paled and was unsure how to answer so he just kept quiet.

Dalziel whispered to Beiste, "It would appear they have been in your uncle's employ all this time. Ludan has also offered coin to the Commissary to find in his favor. Whether the Commissary has accepted is another matter."

"The bastard, he canna get away with this." Beiste was so frustrated.

The crowd mumbled and gave Amelia suspicious looks. Her energy was waning from the proceedings. She knew it was the babe, but she hoped she had enough to at least last the day, she felt so exhausted.

The Queen leaned across to her husband and murmured something in his ear.

The King stood. "I think we should break for rest and refreshments we will meet again before the evening meal." With that, he and the Queen moved to the dais.

Amelia was ushered into a private room by stewards, and Beiste was called to join her. There was a small trundle bed for her to rest on and a servant girl arrived with food and beverages from the Queen's share. Amelia had never felt so grateful for the refreshments and the respite. Beiste sat on the bed, and she sat on his lap as they enjoyed the meal together. Neither of them talking, there was no need. It was enough they were allowed this time to be together.

The Last Witness

THE FOLLOWING DAY IT was their turn to call their witnesses. Amelia stood in the Great Hall once more, except this time the Queen was not present. The proceedings started as usual. Amelia's witnesses were few, but they were honest people. Amelia was tiring under the strain of false accusations. She worried that she might lose everything. She was so close to weeping.

Beiste wanted to slay every man in the room for putting his wife through this ordeal. He could see her looking pale and weary. He had been worried about her these past few days; she seemed to be so sick. He was so grateful to Orla for her constant care of Amelia and for keeping him apprised of her welfare. If they all got through this, he would make sure Orla never wanted for anything for the loyalty and support she gave Amelia.

It seemed as if the Commissary had already decided on Amelia's guilt, for he did not take into account the people who spoke on her behalf. Beiste knew in instances like this, justice was rarely served in Royal Court. This was political and whoever strategized the best, won. He could not bear to think of life without his wife. What they needed was a miracle.

After they had exhausted all their witnesses, Amelia was close to giving up. She knew Ludan's evidence had been strong, even if the witnesses had all lied.

Before the day ended, they had to make one last call for witnesses then the Court would adjourn to decide her fate.

The Commissary called one last time, "Is there anyone else here who can speak to the character of the accused?"

No one came forward. Amelia was downcast until she heard the Queen's voice say loud and clear, "I can speak for her."

Amelia looked up instantly. Beiste also stared at the Queen as if she had grown two heads.

The crowd looked towards the front as Queen Gruoch entered the room. There was a hush. She greeted her husband Macbeth with a kiss, then Amelia watched the Queen slowly walk towards her.

Amelia was so exhausted, but she stood to courtesy.

"Sit down, there is no need," the Queen said.

Amelia sat and looked around in confusion.

The Commissary said, "Your Majesty please explain how you can speak on behalf of this woman."

"I can vouch for her because she saved the life of my grandnephew."

There was more muttering from the crowd. The Queen looked to the back of the hall and said, "I call upon my niece to come forward and explain."

Amelia had no idea who the Queen was referring to, she had never met her before or any of her relations and she certainly had never treated royalty. Like everyone else in the hall, Amelia turned to look to the back of the room. There was a commotion and murmuring as the crowd parted for a woman who would be her last hope.

When the woman finally came into view Amelia gasped in surprise. For there, walking down the aisle was none other than Eliza Kennedy.

Beiste saw the Kennedy woman and almost wept. He remembered her and her son Thomas, the day he saved his wife from attacking Eliza's husband with a broom.

Eliza stepped forward to the dais and in a loud voice addressed the Court. "I second what my aunt the Queen has said. This woman saved my son, Thomas Boite Kennedy even when it meant putting herself in danger."

"Please explain how she saved your son and what methods she used," the Commissary asked.

"I and my guardsman watched her the whole time, and she did not use sorcery only healing knowledge passed to her by her *màthair* who kenned such practices learned from the Abbey. My son Thomas suffered a stomach complaint, Amelia MacGregor found an alternative food source for him, and he is very healthy now."

"How do you ken it wasn't witchcraft?" the Commissary asked.

"Because she consulted a book from Iona Abbey, it was written in Latin, the language of the Church and it set out many healing methods. The method she used has also been used before by religious orders such as monasteries and nunneries."

"Did you see this book?"

"I did. I looked around the cottage while the healer gathered things outside for my son and I came across it. She consulted the book and applied the cure to my son. How can a woman who uses healing practices taught by the Christian church be a witch?" Eliza asked.

Amelia wept with relief.

The crowd hushed and Ludan realized he had lost his battle once more.

Macbeth secretly smiled to himself as the Commissary looked uncertain about what to do. If he ruled with Ludan, he would call the Queen a liar, her niece a liar, and the Christian church practice sorcery.

Macbeth knew what petty jealousies ruled the clans. He liked Beiste MacGregor and would much rather have him as a loyal vassal than his deceitful uncle.

After much debate, the Court ruled Amelia MacGregor was no witch and her husband, Chieftain Beiste MacGregor, was fit to rule his clan.

Ludan lost his temper. "No!" he shouted and lunged at Amelia with a dirk. He was stopped in his tracks when Macbeth stood from his throne and threw his dagger at Ludan's throat. His aim was true and Ludan collapsed in front of Amelia's feet, blood seeping from his neck, but he was still alive.

Guards appeared and carried Ludan away as Macbeth ordered him to be imprisoned in the dungeons. A hush came over the crowd, reminding everyone why they called Macbeth the blood 'Red King.'

With a flick of his wrist, prison guards came forward and detained Elora and Wallace for false testimony. Both began shouting in protest but to no avail. Beiste doubted anyone would see either of them again.

The Royal Send-off

AFTER THE GREAT HALL was cleared and the proceedings completed, Amelia, Orla, and Eliza sat together with the Queen in her solar taking refreshments while Macbeth, Beiste, and Dalziel held council in the King's private chambers.

The Queen was playing with Thomas, who was sitting on her lap and looking every bit a healthy and spoilt baby. The Queen was laughing, and Thomas was giggling at the faces she was pulling.

"I cannot thank you enough, Your Majesty, for your kindness these past two days and you, Eliza, for speaking on my behalf. How can I ever repay you?"

"It is we who should thank you for saving this precious child," the Queen replied. "He has given us so much joy whenever his mother visits."

"Thomas would have died had it not been for your knowledge. I hoped that someday I could repay your kindness and I am glad it came today. Although I am sorry, I looked around your cottage but not sorry I saw the book," Eliza said as she hugged Amelia.

"Mayhap when your babe is born you will come and visit us also Amelia, this place could use the laughter of bairns," the Queen said.

"I am sure I can arrange it," Amelia replied.

AS THEY TOOK THEIR leave, the next day, Amelia and Beiste thanked the royal couple for their hospitality, and bid farewell to Eliza and Thomas.

"We will see you again, my dear. God bless you both," Macbeth said as the couple waved them off.

As they rode away from the castle, Beiste said, "Well wife it seems you have friends in high places. Come, let us go home."

Beiste kissed Amelia deeply and when he gazed upon her countenance, he could not imagine any being on earth lovelier than his wife.

SIX MONTHS LATER, IONA Jonet MacGregor, was born into a Keep filled with her kin. The MacGregors, Macleans, Dunbars, and even the Frasers were there. And when her father saw her for the first time, he thought she was the loveliest being he had ever seen.

Epilogue

MacGregor Keep, Glenorchy, Scotland, 1042

Beiste bathed in the loch after training his men and then made his way to his private chambers to check on Amelia. He found her curled up sleeping peacefully in their large four-poster bed. As he watched, he could not resist brushing the back of his knuckle against her cheek. He bent down and kissed her lips, savoring the sweetness.

She looked exhausted, but still managed a smile in her sleep. Beiste's chest squeezed. He loved this woman more than anything in the world. It almost scared him.

"Beiste?" Amelia asked, still half asleep.

"Aye, sweeting?"

"Please try not to wake the bairns this time."

He suppressed a laugh. "I promise I'll not wake our bairns."

"Good, because if you do, I swear I'll kill you," she replied in a husky voice.

Beiste kissed her forehead as Amelia yawned, snuggling deeper into her pillow, and drifted back to sleep.

Beiste knew he should go back down to the hall and see to his men, but he could not resist taking a quick peek at the nursery. He would be quick and this time he did not have Brodie or Dalziel stomping around the room, fighting over whose turn it was to carry the babe. The ruckus they caused last time resulted in all three men being banished from the nursery. He chuckled at the memory of his feisty wife beating Dalziel and Brodie with a soft toy and threatening to castrate Beiste if he ever woke her son again.

No, there was no way he was waking anyone up this time.

Beiste crept into the adjoining room to peek at his baby son, Colban Gilleain MacGregor. He tucked Colban's blanket in, leaned forward, and kissed his cheek. The baby sighed and Beiste smiled at the overwhelming feeling of love that surged through him. He would never get used to seeing his babe sleeping without a care in the world.

He then looked over to the larger cot on the other side of the room where his two-year-old daughter *should* be, only to find the space empty. *Where had his little warrior disappeared to now?* He was about to go on a hunt when he heard a shuffling noise under Colban's cradle.

"Iona, are you under there?" he whispered.

After a brief pause, he heard a muffled response, "No Da, I'm not."

Beiste chuckled quietly and crouched down, whispering, "Iona, come out from under there now."

His daughter emerged from underneath the crib with a mass of black curls and chubby limbs. She gazed up at him with one green eye and one brown. Holding an index finger to her lips, she said, "Shush, Da, I'm hiding from Ma."

Beiste reached down and picked Iona up, cradling her against him. She immediately wrapped her arms around his neck and kissed his scarred cheek. Beiste choked on the lump in his throat. His daughter was his little warrior who had him wrapped around her little finger, just like her mother. Beiste straightened to stand, holding her firmly in his arms.

"Why are you hiding from your *màthair,* Iona?" he asked, kissing her on the tip of her nose.

"Because Ma doesna want me to wake Colban." She frowned.

"And were you trying to wake him?" Beiste questioned her with one eyebrow raised.

Iona instinctively nodded her head, realizing what she was doing, stopped midway to shake it instead. Her brow furrowed as her dark curly hair bobbed from side to side with the movement. "No, Da, I wasn't."

Beiste bit back a laugh. "Iona, you ken your *màthair* needs her sleep, and if Colban is awake, she's unable to rest?"

"But I just want to play with him Da." She pouted. Then a thought suddenly came to her. She placed both of her hands on either side of Beiste's face and looking straight into his eyes. She pleaded, "Can you wake him, Da?" Her eyes rounded with the exciting possibility. "If you wake him, I will not get into trouble." In her excitement, Iona's leg, which was dangling near the cradle, hit the edge with a jerk, setting it to rock.

As if on cue, Colban opened his eyes and stared up at his father and sister before his face scrunched up, threatening to cry.

Beiste cursed. "Blast!" He set Iona gently to the ground, picked up his son, and began rocking him back and forth.

"Shh son, go back to sleep or your *màthair* will kill me." Desperation set an edge to his voice. Colban whimpered as Beiste increased his rocking. Iona started jumping up and down in excitement. "You did it, Da, you woke him up. Can I play with him now?"

"Keep your voice down. You canna play with him. He needs to sleep."

"But I want to play with him," she whined.

"No, Iona, you canna play with your brother," Beiste stated in a firm voice.

Colban seemed to pick up on the tension and before Beiste could do anything, he let out a loud cry and wailed.

"Blast!" Beiste cursed again.

"Blast!" Iona repeated after him. Beiste stared in shock.

"Iona, you must never let *mamaidh* hear you say that word."

"But you say it, Da?"

"That's different. I'm a chieftain, and I can use bad words."

She looked confused, then shrugged her shoulders and started jumping up and down chanting, "Colban's awake. Colban's awake!"

"Beiste? What is the meaning of this?" Amelia stepped into the room, looking bedraggled and exhausted. She glared at her daughter. "Iona Jonet MacGregor, did you wake your brother?" Amelia placed both her hands on her hips and scowled at the pair.

Beiste and Iona both froze. Then Iona blurted out, "Twas Da, he woke Colban and said blast." With that, she ducked behind her father, wrapping her arms around his leg. She peeked up at Amelia with her vivid eyes.

"Traitor," Beiste muttered under his breath, instinctively clapping one hand over Iona's mouth lest she let out any more damning evidence against him. He rocked a now screaming Colban in his other arm. "I swear Amie twas Iona's fault. She is demon spawn," he said, with a guilty expression on his face.

Amelia took one look at her husband's face, and her ire abated. There he stood, a six-foot-five warrior reduced to a panic-stricken mess. A screaming babe in one arm and a mouthy bairn wrapped around his leg. This was her husband, the *father* of her children, and she loved him even more.

Letting out a deep sigh, Amelia threw her hands up in the air and crossed the room. Unable to put up with the ruckus any longer, she reached out to take Colban.

"Hush little one, tis all right, *mamaidh* is here now," she cooed as Colban immediately settled. Beiste looked relieved. He reached down and picked Iona up. She curled up in his arms and stuck a thumb in her mouth.

"What am I to do with you all?" Amelia shook her head, then leaned across to kiss her daughter. Iona took her thumb out of her mouth and gave her mother a loud smacking kiss on the lips before resting her head back on her father's shoulder.

"I think I need a kiss too, wife." Beiste chided. Amelia stood on tiptoe with Colban cradled between them as Beiste bent his head lower and kissed her soundly.

"Tis a good thing I love you, Husband."

"Not as much as I love you, Wife." He winked.

They settled within an hour, all four in their enormous bed. Beiste and Amelia sat up against the headrest while Iona slept on Amelia's lap and Colban slept on his father's chest.

Amelia sighed with contentment. "Finally, some peace." She rested her head on Beiste's shoulder.

"I love you Amie mine," he said as he kissed her hair. "I love the *teaghlach* you have given me," Looking down at his bairns, he continued, "even if our *nighean* is a hellion like her *màthair*." He reached across, pushing a ringlet away from Iona's face.

"I love you, Husband and our wee bairns, even if our son bellows like his da." She grinned.

Beiste made a mock look of outrage. "I dinnae bellow."

Amelia chuckled, paused for a while as silence descended between them, then she continued. "That day in Dunbar Castle when you chose me to be your betrothed, I never thanked you. You saved my life, Beiste, and gave me a future I could never have dreamed for myself." Amelia smiled up at Beiste, who was gazing at her with intensity.

"No Amie, you saved me. I will always choose you, Love." Beiste's voice was hoarse with emotion and Amelia's eyes glistened with unshed tears as an overwhelming feeling of love passed between them.

Brodie

BRODIE LAY ON THE BED, staring at the ceiling in utter frustration. Beside him lay a very naked, buxom blonde with an equally dissatisfied expression on her face. He should be replete and sated. He should have spent the best night of his life in a euphoric haze of debauchery. But no, he had done nothing of the sort because, for some unknown reason, little Brodie refused to perform. No matter how hard he tried, he failed to become aroused.

"Tis all right, mayhap when you have had some rest we could try again?" the woman beside him asked as she reached for him.

Brodie instinctively rolled out of bed. He knew there was no way he was going through another embarrassing night like that again.

"Ah... no thank you, Felda?"

She glared at him.

"Helda?"

"My name is Zelda!" She pouted.

"Right, my lovely Zelda. I am sorry, I have just had a lot on my mind," Brodie said as he gathered his clothes. He made his farewells, left more than enough coin on the table, mumbled some apologetic words, and exited the cottage.

Feeling annoyed with his predicament, he swore into the night. *It was all that damn wench's fault.* The one who plagued his mind constantly. The one with the big innocent eyes and beautiful tanned skin, skin that glistened in the water when she swam, and pert breasts that could fit comfortably in his hands. Brodie was depraved, he knew it. He had watched her many times swimming in the loch and wanted so much to join her.

Why could he not get her out of his head? Because she was forbidden fruit, that is why. Beiste and Amelia, with their happy little family life, had warned him not to touch her on the pain of death.

It was all her fault. *Orla* the sexy minx, *Orla* the woman whose look could pierce his soul and whose sharp tongue could flay him. He needed a change of scenery. He needed to get far away from here, where she did not haunt his thoughts constantly.

Brodie was still walking and fumbling with his belt buckle when he crashed headlong into someone. He heard a screeched, "Ouch" and then he froze.

Speak of the devil. Brodie just stared at Orla, then wondered what she was doing walking through the woods at this time of the night with an arsenal of weapons. Of all the people to bump into.

Orla blushed when she realised it was Brodie, then she took in the measure of his half-dressed state, and Zelda's cottage not far behind him, and her face went blank.

A part of Brodie wanted to reach out and tumble Orla on the grass and just like that, little Brodie went rock hard in an instant he could barely walk. He needed her to move away, so he verbally lashed out and said, "Watch where you're going, Orphan!"

Brodie saw the flicker of hurt register in her eyes before Orla turned away from him and ran into the woods.

Damn it, he was a bastard. Brodie realised he had two choices. He could forget about Orla, march his sorry ass to the loch and scrub his body of Zelda's cloying scent, or he could find out why the vixen was sneaking about the woods, especially with warnings of raiders about.

Brodie knew there was no actual choice as he took off through the woods in hot pursuit.

THE END

Brodie & Orla's story is up next...
https://elinaemerald.com/books
Sign up for Elina's Newsletter & Free Story
https://dl.bookfunnel.com/aiq0ubhpx6

Buy Direct & Save
https://payhip.com/elinaemerald

Author Notes

Beiste & Amelia

Beiste MacGregor and Amelia Dunbar have rattled around in my head for the past six years. Roaring and bellowing and shouting and yelling and screaming until I finally decided this year to unleash the Beast.

This book took me about four months to write and five and a half years procrastinating about writing it. It was supposed to be a short novella just to get me started, but once I let Beiste out, an entire universe came with him. Before I knew it, I was immersed in a world of Scottish kings, medieval herbal medicines, Viking mix-bloods, the Orkney Isles, the Hebridean Isles, and the language of the Gaels. The little novella turned into a novel because Beiste carries a lot of baggage, and he has a lot of friends.

Historical info and fictional portrayals

A few notes to share regarding my research.

Anyone familiar with Scotland will know that **Glenorchy** is associated with Clan Campbell however, way back in the 1000s, the MacGregors were there, or should I say, they were there first. It is interesting to note that about three hundred years later, the MacGregor name was outlawed. Their descendants became known as 'Children of the Mist.' But that is someone else's story to tell.

Macbeth, the Red King, was a real historical figure, not just a Shakespearean character. From historical accounts, he was apparently a good King, contrary to the play 'Macbeth'. He was well-traveled, highly educated, quite religious, and also a formidable warrior. His policies were considered quite progressive as he pushed for equal inheritance laws for women. He reigned in peace for seventeen years, and during his time, Scotland thrived. He even took a religious pilgrimage to Rome with his wife and his first cousin Thorfinn Sigurdsson, the famous Earl of Orkney.

Gilleain Maclean of 'the Battle Axe' and his three sons really existed, however, in a different time period. But once I read their history well, what can I say?

Maldred Dunbar, King Duncan's brother, was a real person, and some records suggest he became Prince of Cumbria. However, he had sons. The most famous being Gospatrick Earl of Northumbria.

Ealdgyth, Maldred's wife, was the daughter of 'Uhtred the Bold.'

I modeled **Lady Agnes**, Amelia's grandmother, on the famous Countess of Dunbar 'Black Agnes' who defended Dunbar Castle against the English. She was a formidable woman.

Beiste having a bronzed skin tone is something I chose deliberately for him based on research I had come across about Romans and Spanish people settling in Scotland hundreds of years ago, so my little fictional brain decided it was quite possible to have a bronzed highlander in the world.

Gaelic is an actual language and many people in the world speak it, it is part of a rich heritage and culture. I speak two languages other than English. Unfortunately, none of those are Gaelic (I am trying to learn through a duo lingo app, but it is very slow going). So, I tried to keep the Gaelic to a minimum and even the accents as well because I did not want to massacre a beautiful language with my ineptitude.

So, to you, the first-time reader of my debut novel, I **thank you** for taking the time to read it. I hope you enjoyed this story as much as I enjoyed writing it. For all the things you'll find within it you dislike, I will say this. I aim to get better as I hone my craft. After all, ***no one becomes a master of their trade overnight.***

Thank you, God bless, and good night!

Cool links about Scottish history and culture below.

A History of Scotland
https://www.bbc.co.uk/programmes/b00nz3b7

The Highland Murray Pittock
https://www.oxfordbibliographies.com/view/document/obo-9780199846719/obo-9780199846719-0029.xml

A History of everyday life in Medieval Scotland
https://www.jstor.org/stable/10.3366/j.ctt1g09wzn

Iona Abbey and Nunnery – Isle of Iona
https://www.historicenvironment.scot/visit-a-place/places/iona-abbey-and-nunnery/

Black Agnes – Countess Dunbar
https://www.johngraycentre.org/people/heroes/black-agnes-agnes-randolph-countess-dunbar-c1310-1361/

The Real King Macbeth 'The Red King' – bloody prowess.
https://ehistory.osu.edu/biographies/macbeth-macfindlaech
https://www.pressreader.com/uk/all-about-history/20171109/281651075379147

Gaelic for authors
https://gaelic.co/gaelic-for-authors/

Westrayans
https://www.buzzfeed.com/christinekenneally/the-history-of-europe-lies-in-british-peoples-dna

Did you love *Betrothed to the Beast*? Then you should read *Handfasted to the Bear*[1] by Elina Emerald!

Brodie 'The Bear' Fletcher is a ladies' man through and through. A legendary warrior on the battlefield, his conquests in the bedchamber are equally renowned. He is his own man. He belongs to no one. But a trauma from his past has him questioning his life trajectory. As Head Guardsman of the War Band to Chieftain Beiste MacGregor (Book 1), Brodie is often in the company of an infuriating mixed-race bowyer named Orla who challenges him at every turn. With the threat of Viking raiders from the North, Brodie finds himself at the mercy of the very woman who threatens to steal his heart.Orla 'the Orphan' has loved Brodie Fletcher for as long as she can remember, but he never once noticed her. Abandoned on the doorstep of 'Morag the Oracle'

---

1. https://books2read.com/u/49lPLJ
2. https://books2read.com/u/49lPLJ

she was raised with the MacGregor clan. A master huntress and trusted advisor to the chieftain's wife, Orla is a constant thorn in Brodie's side, with her razor-sharp wit and waspish tongue. Everything changes when Jarls from the North stake their claim.

They will all discover firsthand what happens when you poke the Bear.Warning: Brawny alpha males, historical inaccuracies and frivolous entertainment. Not suitable for readers under the age of 18. It contains mature content.

Read more at https://elinaemerald.com/books.

About the Author

Born in the South Pacific, Elina Emerald grew up in a small Australian country town. After graduating from University, she embarked on a short-lived legal career before writing love songs and touring with an indie band. She travelled the world and developed a penchant for researching medieval world history. She now writes Romantic Suspense in Historical, Contemporary and Sci-fantasy genres.

Read more at https://elinaemerald.com/books.